THE PATTERSON WOMEN

THE PATTERSON WOMEN

A Family of Psychopaths

Sara, Kate, and Ann

BRYCE THUNDER KING

Clovercroft Publishing

The Patterson Women: A Family of Psychopaths Sara, Kate, and Ann
Copyright ©2025 Bryce Thunder King

All rights reserved. No part of this book may be reproduced or transmitted in any form or by any means, electronic or mechanical, including photocopying, recording, or by any information storage and retrieval system, without permission in writing from the copyright owner.

Published by Clovercroft Publishing
ClovercroftPublishing.com

Cover Design and Interior Design by Suzanne Lawing

Printed in the United States of America

ISBN: (print) 978-1-956370-94-2

*Special thanks
to
Margie Miller, who urged the completion of this story.*

PROLOGUE

"Ladies, I'm going over to see Mother. I shouldn't be gone long. Meanwhile can I get anything for either of you?" Kate asked, addressing Cynthia and Molly.

"I'll be doing my physical therapy," Molly said.

"Is it okay if I watch TV?" Cynthia asked.

"Of course it's okay! This is your home. You can do whatever you want," Kate said. "When you stay with Ann, that's also your home. All our homes are your homes."

Cynthia giggled. "Okay," she said, dragging the word out and sounding pleased with Kate's response.

Cynthia was befriended by Kate when they were in Nashville Prison for Women. Kate had been sent there after she was convicted of tying her boyfriend to a chair and burning him alive. Cynthia had been stuck there by a judge who should have sent her to a long-term rehabilitation center. Cynthia supported Kate when they were in proximity in the prison. On one occasion, she attacked other prisoners who were harassing Kate which resulted in them being immediately sent to solitary confinement, or the "hole," as they called it in the prison.

In her mid-twenties, Cynthia was a short, stocky person with dirty looking blonde hair. Her hands and arms were short, plump, and unusually strong. Her light blue eyes were her greatest asset. They sparkled with any change in light, and one was immediately fascinated when they confronted her.

Molly had become part of the family because of her association with Ann. Several months earlier, Ann had been a paid sniper for an underground organization with headquarters in New York City.

After performing several jobs at the direction of the kingpin of the firm, Ann decided she wanted to quit. An order immediately went out to kill her.

As part of her efforts to escape the killers, she left her telephone, identification, and all personal effects at home and fled to the riverbank of the Cumberland River. There she met Molly, who lived on the streets and on the riverbank.

Molly had little education. She had learned to survive on her wits and without any personal resources. The weather had taken a toll on her appearance although her dark eyes were immediately noticeable. Her dark hair was tangled; her skin and lips were dry; she was so suntanned that one could not guess her ethnicity. She was average height, around five feet, three or four inches tall. Even with her unkempt appearance, one would guess that she was in her mid-twenties.

Kate left the house and walked to Sara's house next door where Ann joined them moments later. Each woman owned their home, all of which were in Hermitage, TN, approximately fifteen miles from Nashville. Sara was wealthy, having invested the profits from Sara's Kitchen, a café she owned in Hermitage, Tennessee. She had retired many years earlier and turned the café over to Kate, who was now following Sara's practice of investing. Ann was the wealthiest, having earned millions of dollars in her side gig as a sniper.

"Good morning," Sara said cheerfully. She embraced Kate and then Ann. "I've called this family meeting to discuss the proposition proposed by Detective...well, now Police Chief Martin."

It was quite a sight to see the three women together in the living room which had hardwood floors partially covered with red Persian rugs. Sara and Kate sat on a dark brown leather couch, and Ann sat in a matching side chair.

They represented three generations: Sara was the mother of Kate, and Kate was the mother of Ann. Each of them was approximately five feet eight inches tall; each of them had red hair that sparkled when reflecting rays of sunlight struck the hair; each of them lacked the gene that allows for conscience and compassion.

Death was an art with them. When Kate was a young child, Sara used the roots from water hemlock plants to poison her husband's tea. Sara told Kate that her father would get sick at the dining room table and for her to disregard his illness. Kate was to sit still and show no emotion. Sara would go through all the motions of calling an ambulance and the police after the father perished at the table.

"About us being cops…well, in our case super cops?" Ann said.

Sara and Kate laughed.

"Quite a proposition, don't you think?" Sara said, looking at Kate and Ann.

"Are you seriously thinking about it, Mother?" Kate asked.

"Well yes, I'm thinking. I'm thinking about what he proposed," Sara said. Then she looked at Kate and Ann as if she were looking for help as to how to address them.

Feeling that she should come to Sara's rescue, Ann turned to Kate and said, "Well, we've been everything else, Mother. Why not be a cop?"

"Whoa! Now you're sounding serious. You're telling me the Patterson women are thinking about donning cop caps and fighting crime?" Kate said.

"Mother, I think the chief was talking about hard-core stuff. We'd be assigned the toughest of the tough," Ann said, looking at her mother, Kate.

Kate glanced at Sara then at Ann, her eyes rolling from one person to the other. Her cheeks flexed tightly. "Really?" she finally said.

There was silence for an uncomfortable time. Then Kate said, "Okay, okay, let's do it. Hold up your hands and repeat after me."

Sara and Ann laughed.

"Mother, this could be dangerous, and it might be physical," Kate said, looking at Sara.

"My dear daughter, I can run as fast as you; I can lift as much as you; my seeing, my hearing, and all other senses are perfect. I'm willing, and I'm ready. I think this might be a lotta fun," Sara said. Then she formed circles of both hands, put them to her face, and pretended to be looking at Kate and Ann through binoculars.

Kate moved her head from one side to the other. Then she said to Ann, "Sweetheart, do you want to participate in this crazy scheme?"

"Like Grandmother said, this could be a lotta fun…like throwing rings around bottles at a carnival," Ann said.

"Or pulling those little swimmy things outta the water at the carnival," Sara said.

They all laughed.

"So, we have a lot to talk about," Sara said. "We need to decide the terms of our engagement; we need to agree on pay; we need to decide the involvement of Molly and Cynthia; we need to know if Kate and Ann can neglect their work."

CHAPTER 1

Someone knocked on the front door.

"That should be the chief. I'll get it," Kate said. She walked to the door and opened it.

"Good afternoon, Chief. Come in."

"Thank you," he said, stepping inside and following Kate to the living room. "This time I think I know everyone here. You're Cynthia, and as I remember you're Molly."

"Good memory," Molly said.

"Still don't like you," Cynthia said.

The chief looked at Cynthia. Then he said, "I'm sorry. Maybe in the days ahead we can be friends."

Cynthia crossed her arms quickly and huffed audibly. From her experience with enforcement officers and prison guards, she was immediately offended with any interaction between her and the enforcement community.

"Are we going to be here long enough that I can have a cup of tea?" Chief Martin asked.

"We might. You know where everything is," Kate said.

The chief went to the kitchen and made tea. Then he returned to the living room where Sara, Kate, Ann, Cynthia, and Molly waited.

"This is really good tea. You probably have the best tea I've ever tried or ever heard of," the chief said.

"Thank you. We have our own special blend. We pride ourselves in great tea," Kate said.

Sara's cheeks relaxed, quickly forming a hint of a smile—probably remembering that she poisoned her husband and the mayor.

"Sara, you called me from a landline telephone inviting me to come by, so here I am."

"I did. We wanted to talk about your proposition," Sara said.

"Are we all going to participate?" the chief asked and then swept his arm out to indicate everyone in the room.

"Everyone is a participant," Sara said.

"So what do you have in mind?"

"We'll accept your proposal to be cops only to apprehend the offenders your department has closed out to cold files. We'll be completely independent of the police department, and we'll work without interference from them. We'll work subject to conditions I will relate, if you're interested."

"You'll accept!" the chief said loudly. Then he grabbed his lips. "Whew! I burned my lips. I wasn't ready for that," he said. "Okay, I'm ready. The conditions?"

"None of us will ever be contacted by telephone, text, Twitter, X, Facebook, Instagram, postal mail, or any other form of communication. Contact will be by word of mouth. When we have something to report, one of us will use a landline to call your office phone and say 'meeting' and then hang up. That will be your clue to come to Kate's home for a meeting.

"When you arrive, you will deposit all your gear in a basket, and it will be stored in a closet away from our meeting.

"You will be wanded all over, including your crotch and backside.

"Does that mean we don't trust you? It means you can think whatever you want to think.

"You will provide a list of addresses of your immediate family, your siblings, your parents, and your in-laws. If you cross us and we wind up in your net, we will destroy all your relatives. You will survive for ten days. Then you will join your family.

"If you plan to entrap us, and let's say you have all of us in custody, you might think that all is well. I assure you that all will not be well. An unknown force would immediately be called into play.

"You will deposit one hundred thousand into a corporation whose name is CWC, Inc."

"CWC? What does that stand for?" the chief asked.

"Cause we care."

The chief smiled. "Anything else?"

"You will provide five names of the baddest individuals that you have not apprehended and you believe you'll not be able to apprehend. We will apprehend the individuals any way we see fit. You will never direct, suggest, criticize, evaluate, or provide any commentary on the manner and result of our apprehension. You may advertise, boast, use the media, and take any credit for the capture that you see fit, but you will never ever reveal that the apprehension was done by none other than yourself.

"After our apprehension of each of the first five, which evidence will be provided to you without any doubt, you'll deposit one hundred fifty thousand in the corporate account.

"Those will be our conditions for now except for weapons. You will provide us with three AR-15s with one thousand rounds of ammunition and five nine-millimeter revolvers along with one thousand rounds of ammunition."

"Why so many rounds of ammunition?" the chief asked.

"Training," Sara said. "And one more thing…a cell phone in the state's name."

"I thought we weren't communicating?" the chief said.

"It's to take a picture of the individuals we apprehend."

"You're not just going to turn them over to us?"

"Oh, we'll turn them over, but you may have to pick them up somewhere."

"Any other requirements?"

"Those are the requirements that will get us started," Sara said.

"There is one thing that I'm not comfortable with, and that is my family. This is a business proposition to which my family is not a part."

"Chief, there is no reason on earth that we should trust you, and we do not. If our requirements are not met, our offer to help you apprehend some bad individuals is off the table."

"No, no, I'm sure we can work something out," the chief said. Then he twisted and turned in his chair for several moments.

From the very beginning of Sara's discussion with the chief, the only thing that moved on the other four women's faces was the blinking of their eyes. Their cheeks were static, their hands didn't move, and their legs were motionless.

"Well, I must admit I need you," the chief said. "The amount of money you're asking for is four times what I had budgeted, and the amount of ammunition you're asking for is like arming an army. I'll have to work it out, but I'll have a contract ready in a day or two."

"Oh, no! No contract. This is a handshake agreement," Sara said.

The chief looked at Sara as if he hadn't heard her correctly. "You don't want a contract?"

"No, no contract. We trust you, but we don't trust you. As far as money, we're going to save the state five times what you would spend in the court system if you get my drift."

"Fair enough. It'll take a few days to secure the weapons, but why don't I see you Monday…here at the same location?"

"We'll be here," Sara said.

"I'll bid you ladies goodnight," the chief said. He stepped outside the front door.

"Ladies, it looks like we're in the cop business," Sara said. Then her cheeks widened in a giant smile, and her green eyes sparkled like polished emeralds.

"Right!" Kate said loudly. Then she rolled her eyes to show her disbelief in their involvement in such a scheme.

Ann and Molly laughed.

Cynthia was quiet, apparently confused about who was doing what.

"Okay, time for a family meeting," Sara said, her voice filled with enthusiasm.

"What now, Mother?" Kate said, her voice still sounding as if she could not believe the entire affair.

"We need an accountant in the family; we need a business law major in the family; and we need a politician in the family. So what about Molly?"

"Me?" Molly said. Then she pointed her index finger toward her chest.

"Yes, you. Don't you want to be a big shot in the family?"

"I do, of course…"

"Great! We have to decide where you will excel. Will it be Belmont, Vanderbilt, or another college?" Sara asked.

"Miss Patterson…" Molly said, and then her voice drifted away.

"My name is Sara to you and to all the other ladies in this household," Sara said.

"Okay, Sara. Everybody knows I never graduated from high school."

"Well, then we'll have to get you graduated."

"Mother, have you asked Molly if she wants to go to school?" Kate asked.

Sara moved her head back as if the question had shocked her. "Why, no, I haven't asked. Is it a good time now?"

"Molly's still here, so this may be the time."

"Molly, I'm so sorry. Sometimes I am so impulsive. Please forgive me."

"Of course," Molly said, "and you don't haf to ask me. I would like to go to school. I've always wanted to be a little smart…"

Ann laughed. Then it became contagious as Kate and Sara joined in. Cynthia giggled, and then she laughed.

"I'm sorry," Ann said. "I just had a case of the giggles."

"The joke's mine," Molly said. "I wanted to sound like I'm in need."

Ann laughed again. "You're in need all right. Anyone that would jump off a barge into the Cumberland River is surely in need."

Everyone laughed.

"Okay," Sara said. "So, it's okay if we get you graduated from high school?"

"Yes, ma'am. It's more than good, but I also want to help you with the cop thing."

"You will! You will, of course!" Sara said.

"Am I going to be a cop?" Cynthia asked.

"Why, of course. We couldn't leave you out, could we ladies?"

Both Kate and Ann assured Cynthia that she would be part of their new adventure.

"Ladies, we'll be talking among ourselves for the next few days, but we'll all meet the chief Monday night."

CHAPTER 2

"I must admit I'm beginning to share some of your excitement, Mother. This could turn out to be a conversation piece. Oh, there's Ann, Molly, and Cynthia coming up the steps. I'll let them in," Kate said. She hurried to the door and opened it.

"Okay, where's the chief?" Ann said in a husky voice.

Molly and Cynthia giggled.

"We're ready to get our cop caps and go after the bad guys," Ann said.

"You gals are just full of it tonight," Sara said. "You haven't been sipping on the juice, have you?"

"Why Grandmother Sara! How could you have such a thought?" Ann said. "Hey, there's the chief's car. He just parked. Everyone be on your best behavior."

Cynthia giggled. "I sure don't want to go to the pokey," she said.

"I'm not going to rush to the door when he knocks," Kate said. "We don't want him to think that we're getting excited about this thing, so let's all sit as if we are the coolest ladies he's ever seen."

Everyone took a seat and waited for the chief. A few seconds passed. Then there was a knock on the door.

Kate looked at all the women, held her seat for a few moments, then walked to the door and opened it. "Good evening, Chief," she said. "Come in."

"Good evening, Kate. Good evening, Sara. Good evening, Ann. Good evening, Molly. Good evening, Cynthia. How is everyone?"

"We're fine," Sara said. "Would you like some tea?"

"I believe I would. I'll get it if you don't mind. I'm very familiar with the kitchen."

"Of course, Chief," Sara said.

The chief prepared a cup of tea and returned to the family room. "Ladies, I have some great news," he said, "but before I rattle on, does anyone have any questions or want to share any information with the group?"

"Ladies, we're ready to listen to the chief, aren't we?" Sara said.

"I think we're all ready to listen," Kate said as she looked at each individual.

"Okay, you demanded a list of my closest blood relatives, and I have it here," Chief Martin went on. "You also asked for a cell phone, and I have that too. I brought a wand for you to use, and I brought a basket for my gear. I'm also ready to deposit funds into CWC, Inc.

"For the weapons and ammo, I've asked a contractor to build a concrete bunker behind Sara's house because she has a large back yard, and the bunker would be camouflaged and inconspicuous. There would be a digital lock, and only the family would know the combination. Is it okay if we do that with your yard, Sara?"

"Why a bunker?" Sara asked.

"To get those items outta your house. It's a real important safety measure. It'll also keep the items away from potential intruders in your house."

Sara looked at him for a moment and said, "Would you remove the bunker if I ever decided to sell my property?"

"Of course."

Sara looked at Kate and Ann, who didn't offer any advice. "Well, it does sound like a good idea. Go ahead with it. I have no objections."

"Good. We will install six cameras around your property, and you will have monitors for each camera inside your house. If a camera detects any movement in the yard, a chime will emit from the monitor."

"When will construction start?"

"Tomorrow morning at seven o'clock. That okay?"

"Sounds good. I'll have coffee ready."

"That is excellent, Sara! That is excellent! Do we have a handshake deal?"

There was silence for a few moments, then Sara said, "Ladies, why don't we adjourn to the kitchen?" Then she got up and walked toward the kitchen.

Each person looked at her, then got up and followed.

"Ladies, as senior in our family, I thought I would take the lead and call us together."

"Mother, you should take the lead. You're the one that created this family. Don't you agree, Ann?" Kate said.

"Absolutely. We'll follow you anywhere, Grandmother."

Sara smiled. "All right. Kate, may I have a blank sheet from your notebook?"

"Here you go. I believe you'll want scissors, and you'll probably want a pen."

"You're so perceptive," Sara said. She took the sheet of paper and cut it into five pieces and gave a piece to each person.

"Ladies, we're going to have an election, and your vote will be unknown. Simply write yes or no to start this adventure or turn it down. I'll vote and then pass the pen to Kate."

"I have to stay out," Cynthia said.

"What do you mean, you have to stay out?" Kate said.

"'Cause I don't know how…I don't know how you all want to vote," Cynthia said.

"Honey, if you want to have some fun and be a cop, then vote yes. If you think it'd be dull, then vote no," Kate said.

"Fun, yes. Dull, no. Okay."

Everyone marked their paper and turned them in to Sara for the verdict.

"Okay, ladies, I have the votes, and I have the result," Sara said.

"Well, Mother, let's have it," Kate said.

"Yeah, c'mon, Grandmother. We're waiting. The suspense is up to here," Ann said, holding her hand up to her neck.

Sara laughed. "So, everyone is ready?"

"Yes, yes," everyone said in unison.

"Okay, okay. Let me add the tote again. I surely would not like to make an error."

Loud sighs followed.

"Okay, I have verified the vote and reported it to the proper authorities. The vote happens to be unanimous!"

Ann jumped from her chair and danced up and down. "We're gonna be cops! We're gonna be cops!" she shrieked. "I voted yes, and if the vote is unanimous then everyone else voted yes!"

Sara smiled. "Like she says, ladies, we're going to be cops."

Ann continued to dance up and down. Her face had a giant smile as her head bobbed in concert with her dancing legs.

"Cynthia, get up, girl!" Molly said, her voice loud and excitable. "You're goin' to miss the party."

Cynthia looked at Molly. Her cheeks were tight, and she looked confused. "How can there be a party when we're goin' to be cops?" she asked.

Ann stopped immediately. She moved closer to Cynthia. "We're not going to have a party, Cynthia. I was just acting silly."

"Ladies let's go meet the chief," Sara said.

The mood in the room changed immediately. All the frivolity was replaced with solemnity. They walked quickly to meet the chief, then formed a half-circle in front of him.

He looked at each one of them but remained silent.

"Chief, we took a vote…"

"Well?"

"The majority voted to accept your offer."

"The majority?"

"Yes, the majority, and the majority rules in our family."

"I'm delighted! I'm delighted more than I can say!" he said, then he shook hands with each of the five women.

"Chief, you said you would provide a list of five individuals that we're to apprehend," Sara said.

"Indeed, I did. I have them right here," he said. He opened his leather case and pulled out several pieces of paper. "I'll start with this one. His name is Herman Alvin Stone, alias 'Big Al.' He's holed up in the mountains behind Crab Orchard."

"Where they mine those beautiful flat rocks?" Kate asked.

"The same," the chief said. "Herman, or Big Al, went on a shooting spree at a church. He killed twelve of the parishioners then the minister. We hunted him for weeks. Then we got a tip that he was hiding out in the mountains…had a cabin, had a rifle to kill for food, and had an uncanny ability to stay outta sight.

"We sent three of our best to hunt him down. One was a woman. She had reached the rank of captain and was highly decorated. She sadly stepped in one of his animal traps which nearly severed her leg. It didn't take long for Herman to find her. He raped her, beat her, and then slit her throat.

"He then proceeded to kill the other two officers. We then sent two helicopters to flush him out. He lured the 'copters into an area which apparently had dried leaves, grass, and other debris. The pilots were talking with our control tower and explaining how Big Al was running one way and then backtracking into the same area. Somehow, he ignited the entire area, and the fire was so intense that it created an updraft so powerful that it brought both 'copters down. Of course, it killed both pilots and four passengers. We couldn't convince the state to send in the National Guard, so we gave up. After that, no one could be convinced to go after him. He has a rap sheet three miles long."

"Do you have a picture of him?" Ann asked.

"I do. The problem is that it's three years old. One of the officers got a shot of him with his bodycam."

"We can work with that," Sara said. "Who's next?"

"Okay, this guy's handle is 'Pinkie.' He specializes in robbing small-town banks. His last job didn't go exactly as planned, and he shot two employees. His real name is Bobby Glen Getty. He has a large black mole in the middle of his forehead. It really stands out. This picture was taken four years ago when he killed the bank employees."

"Where does he hang out?" Kate asked.

"He has some relatives south of Triune, Tennessee. He slips in and outta his uncle's house, but he's also been seen in West Point, Mississippi. The addresses are on this page."

"Two down and three to go," Sara said.

"Number three is an extremely dangerous man," the chief said. "He was convicted for five rapes, but on the way from the courthouse to the jailhouse he escaped. That was two years ago, and he hasn't been seen since. He had a farm about halfway between Murfreesboro and Franklin, but we wore out the farm and the area around the farm with stakeouts. His name is Randy Millington."

"You have to have a picture of him," Ann said.

"We certainly do. These pictures as you can see are his mug shots before he went to trial. He had a wife, but she's in the women's prison for obstruction of justice, tampering with evidence, and blackmail."

"Blackmail?" Kate said.

"Yes. It seems one of the women he raped was the wife of a politician who was at a house where she shouldn't have been. Susan, Randy's wife, overheard Randy talking to his attorney and learned about the politician's wife. Later, Susan tells Randy that she's going to the politician to tell him the whole story unless Randy gives her money."

"Quite a woman," Kate said.

"Yeah, birds of a feather flock together," the chief said.

"Okay, we've heard about Big Al, Pinkie, and Randy. Who's next?" Sara asked.

"This one is a child molester," the chief said. "His last name is Robie. He uses several names: Trey, Buddy, Izzie, Jeff, just to name a few. The only picture we have is six years old. Our photo guys have aged the picture to show what they think he looks like today. So here it is," he said, and then he showed the picture to everyone. "He was last seen going into one of the nightclubs on Broadway. That was many years ago. We want him badly. Oh! He has a sister in West Nashville. Her name and address are in the package."

"All right. Who is number five?" Sara asked.

"Number five is a woman. Her name is Sally Sue Cross Bottoms. She shot her husband when he came home from work. Before that, she drowned her two youngest children and suffocated her other daughter, age ten. We think she's in Tennessee, but we have no leads. Her picture and newspaper clippings are in the package.

"That's all I have. I'm sure you'll have questions and a need for additional information as you begin to work on these cases. I'm always available. Any questions for now?"

Sara looked at each of the women who stated they had no questions.

"Well then, I'll be going. I'll see you tomorrow when they start the bunker."

"Good night, Chief," Sara said.

Each person said goodnight to the chief.

"Kate and Ann, may I see you in the kitchen?" Sara said.

A puzzled look crossed each of their faces.

After some hesitation, Kate said, "Let's go, daughter. Your grandmother has summoned us."

"You go first," Ann said.

When they got to the kitchen, Sara stood near the island counter. She held a ceramic black-and-white drink cup. Then she turned it upside down. Three black marbles and three white marbles rolled out onto the counter. She gave one black marble and one white marble to Kate and then gave one of each to Ann. She was left with one of each which she clutched in her hand.

"Ladies, when we refer to a person that we plan on apprehending, let's refer to that person as a 'Mark.' So we presently have Mark One, Mark Two, Mark Three, and so on.

"Once we decide on the mark, we're going to vote. This black and white cup will always be here. It is never to be moved. From the information we have on a mark, deposit either a black or white marble in the cup. No one will ever know how each of us voted unless it's unanimous. Then we'll know, of course.

"The black marble signifies that the mark is not to survive, and the white marble signifies the mark deserves a second chance. Is that clear, or have I bungled the whole story?"

"Oh, it's perfectly clear, Mother," Kate said.

"Yes, you were right on point, Grandmother," Ann said.

"I have a question, though," Sara said.

"Ann, I think we better sit down," Kate said.

"Since we're about to enter the legal side of society, and I say that with tongue in cheek, would it be a good thing if we referred to each other with a code name?" Sara asked.

"Grandmother, I think that would be confusing. I'd wind up calling you Dave or Steve or some weird name that'd get us shot."

"You may be right. What about this? Rather than refer to me as Grandmother or Mother, just call me Sara. That way if you and I meet up with Big Al, and you call me Grandmother, I won't be the first one he tries to choke."

Ann and Kate laughed.

"Okay, Sara, is Big Al our first mark?" Kate asked.

"He is unless someone has an objection."

"Big Al it is," Kate said.

"Then it's time to vote," Sara said. "Who's first?"

"I'll volunteer," Ann said.

"Okay, you know where the voting box is," Sara said. "We'll give you some privacy while you vote."

After they had left the room, Ann's eyebrows rose instantly, causing her eyes to look larger than normal. She jumped up and rushed to the island counter and placed a marble in the ceramic cup. "Next," she called loudly, then joined Sara and Kate.

"My turn," Kate said, then she went to the kitchen, stayed for a few moments, and returned. "Your turn, Sara."

Sara smiled, then went to the kitchen, stayed a few moments, and returned. "I voted and then I tallied the votes. They were all black."

Kate looked at Ann. "I suppose we go to work."

"I'll make arrangements at the produce company," Ann said. "After all, I am the CEO."

"Ladies, there's one more meeting I'd like to have, and this one includes Molly and Cynthia," Sara said.

"Well, let's go join them," Kate said.

They joined Molly and Cynthia.

"Ladies, our first assignment is to apprehend Big Al. We need a plan of attack. Any suggestions?"

"Sara, what if Molly and I go talk to the locals?" Ann asked. "The first question would be if anyone knows anything about a cabin in the woods. Has anyone seen Big Al? How do we dress going into the woods?"

"And what creatures are in the woods?" Molly said.

Everyone laughed.

Ann laughed the loudest, and then she said, "You got that right! What kind of creatures are there…besides Big Al, of course."

"Both of you have a great idea and an excellent starting point, don't you think so, Kate?"

"I do, Moth…that is, Sara."

Sara smiled. "Okay, the concrete guys are coming tomorrow. Ann, when do you think you and Molly can go to Crab Orchard?"

Ann looked at Sara, then Molly. "Can you travel after your surgery? Doctor Phillips worked on your pancreas, and that's pretty serious," she asked.

"I'm almost healed. I'm ready for a trip to the country," Molly said. "Oh, I will check with the doc though."

"Leave day after tomorrow?" Ann asked.

"At seven?" Molly asked.

"Seven's good."

"There's another subject," Sara said.

"Another one?" Kate said, her voice sounding somewhat exasperated.

"Yes, we need to make a master record of people we trust. In the days ahead, we may need it as a reference for things that we need to get done or maybe help with some issue. I have this notebook which will contain our entries. Does anyone want to start the list?" Sara asked.

"I'll start it," Ann said.

Sara looked at Ann with a quizzical look. "Okay," she said.

"Benjamin," Ann said.

"Benjamin?" Sara said. "What's his last name?"

"Just Benjamin. That's the only name I have."

"Honey, tell us about Benjamin," Kate said.

"He's a dockworker down at the riverfront."

"A dockworker?" Kate said.

"Yes, Kate. It's a long story but trust me. He's a good contact that should go on the list."

"Benjamin it is," Sara said.

"Doctor Phillips should go on the list. Don't you think, Ann?" Molly said.

"Doctor Phillips should absolutely be on the list," Ann said.

"Isn't he the one that did your surgery?" Kate asked, looking at Molly.

"Yes, and he's a good doctor. Someone we should know."

"We all know him," Sara said. "He's eaten at the café many times. Anyone else?"

"Well, Dave, my manager," Ann said.

"That's a good choice," Kate said.

"Anyone else?" Sara said.

"Sara, I'll mill it over at the café and give you some names a little later," Kate said.

"Good idea. I'll make my list, also. Any other subjects, ladies?" Sara asked.

"Not for us. We're headed home," Ann said.

Everyone said goodnight. Then Ann, Molly, and Cynthia left.

"I'll walk you home, Mother," Kate said.

Sara smiled.

Two mornings later, Molly joined Ann in the living room.

"Good morn', girl. I brought the coffee," Molly said. "This is just like ol' times. Another adventure. Hopefully I won't do somethin' like I did when I jumped off the barge."

Ann laughed. "We're just going to talk with the local people," she said.

From Hermitage, they drove east for nearly two hours until they reached the exit to Crab Orchard.

"Here we are," Molly said.

After taking the exit, Ann said, "Looks like the town's over on my left. Have you ever been here?"

"Passed by goin' somewhere."

"Well, we're really going to have a new adventure, aren't we? We could get a drink at that store there, but we'll get it on the way out so we can stop in Crossville for a rest stop, if you know what I mean."

Molly laughed. "I got it," she said. "Hey, what about them guys at the rock place?"

"Good idea. Here we go," Ann said. She pulled into an empty space and parked. Pallets of stone occupied the area. They got out of the car, and a large man began walking immediately toward the car. He wore jeans that were covered with dust, and his shirt was wet with perspiration. He was tanned dark from working in the sun. His jaw was rounded and his cheekbones were wide and strong looking.

"Can I help you, ladies?" he asked.

"We were just admiring your stones. It must have taken forever to cut these so beautifully," Ann said.

"Oh, we don't cut these. Mother Nature made them. You see, thousands of years ago, debris was deposited that formed a layer and thousands of years passed until the same process happened again. These beautiful, flat stones come out of the ground just as you see them. We do cut some when a customer wants a particular size. Now, can I help you with some stone?"

"You have been so nice to take this time with us, mister..."

"Just call me Clay."

"Okay, Clay. Can you give us just a few more minutes?"

"Let me get a drink. Do you ladies want a drink?"

"Oh, no, thanks. We just had one."

Clay walked to a building and then returned with a glass of water. "What's on your minds, ladies?"

"We were told this was a great place to hike into the mountains and just wanted to know if we can talk with the local people to find out if that's true."

"Ladies, unless you are an experienced mountain person, these are mountains you want to stay away from. I have two sons who have practically lived in the mountains since they were born. They go hunting for wild pigs just about every weekend."

"Wild pigs?" Ann asked.

"Wild pigs, wild hogs. You get 'em hemmed up, you're in trouble. They move fast, and their tusks could tear you to pieces."

"Whoa! Do they just attack you at will?"

"No, no, they try to avoid humans. Just don't go near their young or try to corner them."

"That's good to know. Just exactly what varmints are in the woods?"

"Rattlesnakes, copperheads, coyotes, bobcats, bats, flying squirrels, hawks, and all the ordinary animals like rabbits, squirrels, and skunks."

"Quite a buffet," Ann said.

"Yeah," Clay said. "One of my sons spotted a black bear last year. That's pretty rare, but there are quite a few north of Crossville."

"That's certainly good to know. One more question...?"

"Go ahead."

"Have your sons or anyone else spotted a cabin back in the woods?"

"Funny you should ask. About the same time my son saw the bear, he also spotted a cabin. He also saw a huge man going in the cabin. He didn't know if the man lived there or was just passing through."

"Where in the woods did he see the cabin?"

"Ladies, are you really lookin' for a hiking trail, or are you making a movie?"

Both Ann and Molly looked at him for a moment, then they burst out laughing. Ann placed her right hand on Clay's shoulder and, once she stopped laughing, she said, "Movie makers we're not. We're just ladies that are lookin' for a hiking place."

Clay's cheeks relaxed, and then he smiled. "Whew!" he said. "You had me scared for a minute. Okay, I'll try to help you. When you turned off the interstate, you came down to that intersection," he said, pointing toward the intersection. "Then you turned left on this road which is US 70. When you decide to hike, and I'd suggest different clothing, instead of turning left, go straight ahead. Drive a short distance, and you'll see a house on the right side of the road that has a front made of these flat stones. That's my house. When you're lookin' straight on at it, look to your left, and you'll see a car-width trail that goes into the mountains. You have a good path for about a mile, and then it gets pretty rugged. Will that help?"

"Clay, you have taken a lot of time with us. You haven't the faintest idea who we are, and you have neglected your business. We thank you, we thank you, we thank you."

"Well, you are respectable-looking ladies, and I am pleased to help. If I can help you in the future, let me know."

"Clay, can I put that down in my book of people that are willing to help? Can I put down, 'call Clay if you have a problem?'"

"You shore can!"

"Great. There are five of us in our clan. Do you mind if the whole family trudges by your house?"

"Anytime you want…night or day. If you want a cold drink, just knock on the door."

"We just might do that. You've been a gentleman, and with that we must go. My name is Ann, and this is Molly. I'm going to text my phone number to you if you need to reach me."

"That's great," Clay said. "My number's 931-555-5555."

Ann texted her number to Clay. "Okay, you should be getting that soon. We'll say goodbye for now. Thank you for your great hospitality."

"See you, ladies."

They got into the car and started toward the interstate. There was silence until they had driven at least five miles on the interstate.

"Well, let's see how many ways there are to die—get bitten by a rattlesnake or, let's try the copperhead," Ann said. "Then, we could always get eaten by the bear. Two or three coyotes would do the trick. And, of course, let's don't forget the wild hogs. So, what'll it be? Such a choice!"

"You forget Big Al." Molly burst out laughing.

"This cop business could get interesting," Ann said.

"You ain't kiddin' about that," Molly said.

"I have to go to the produce shop when we get back. Do you want me to drop you at my place?"

"No, if you don't mind, drop me at the café. I'll help Kate."

"Okay, tell Mother…Kate, that is, that I'm bringing sandwiches and fixings to her house tonight about seven. We are to report our findings and discuss Big Al.

"By the way, if you didn't get the message, we're to call Kate by her name and Sara by her name—no mother or grandmother."

"So be it."

Ann drove to the café and dropped Molly off. Then she drove to her produce company and put out business fires until five-thirty. She called a sub shop and ordered subs for pickup. After that, she went home, changed clothes, picked up the subs, drove to Kate's house, got out of the car, and went inside. Everyone had arrived before her.

"Okay, gang, the food truck has arrived. Wow! I bet you sneaked into the café and made these," Kate said.

"No, Mother, you were out of lettuce, so I just went down the street and spent my money elsewhere," Ann said.

"Listen to her! She owns a produce company, and she forgets to bring lettuce," Kate said.

Everyone laughed.

"Okay, ladies, let's eat, and then Ann and Molly have a report for us. The bunker is in, by the way, and we have weapons and ammunitions."

After a great deal of bantering among the ladies, and once they finished eating, Sara said, "Okay, ladies, if there are no objections, we'll have our first strategy meeting. Ann and Molly, the floor is yours."

"What did you tell 'em so far, Molly?" Ann asked.

"Oh, girl, not a word. I'm leaving this story to you."

Sara's and Kate's eyebrows rose, and they stared at Ann. Cynthia's expression didn't change. She seemed confused about the whole affair.

"Fellow justice facilitators, it is my pleasure to report the following—"

She was interrupted when everyone laughed.

"She was always timid as a child…never spoke out," Kate said, referring to Ann.

Cynthia giggled.

"Better remember who your best friend is, girl," Ann said, a mischievous smile showing on her face as she looked at Cynthia.

"You're my very best friend…well, one of them," Cynthia said, her voice humble-sounding.

"Of course we're friends," Ann said. "Okay, back to justice stuff. Molly and I drove over to Crab Orchard. We met a guy named Clay, which should be added to our list of contacts. He owns a stone lot . . . sells those beautiful flat stones that were formed thousands of years ago, and they come straight out of the ground looking like a polished, flat piece of beauty.

"He spent half the afternoon talking with us. He was patient and answered all our questions. He also lives right beside the trail that goes to the woods.

"One of Clay's sons saw a cabin about a mile and a half back in the mountain. He also saw a large man going into the cabin. My bet would be that was Big Al, and he calls the cabin home.

"The obstacles are the following in no priority order.

"The mountain has rattlesnakes, copperheads, coyotes, wild hogs, bobcats, foxes, bats, flying squirrels, and on top of that…a bear. So how do you take down a bear?"

"Pepper spray," Cynthia said.

Everyone burst out laughing.

"By the way, Clay said to feel free to go by his house any time. Even invited us in," Ann said. "For the coming days, Kate, Molly, and I will locate the cabin and then hide in the brush and watch for Big Al to appear. At least that's my suggestion.

"We'll all wear those snake protector things on our legs and arms, wear high-top leather shoes, and leather gloves.

"Molly, do you know what we do if we run upon a bear?" Ann asked.

"Run!" Molly said loudly.

"And get eaten," Ann said. "A bear can run close to thirty miles an hour. We're taking walking sticks, and I'm taking a bag of rocks. If we see a bear, we'll back up slowly to see if the bear will go away. Don't look at the bear's eyes. If the bear approaches us, jump on the nearest rock, stump, or anything that makes you look taller. Raise your hands and arms in the air and make all the motions you can. We have to try to refrain from yelling because we could alert Big Al.

"I doubt the wild pigs or hogs will cause us any problem," she said. "For coyotes, we'll each take a pellet pistol. If things get really rough, we'll each have a nine-millimeter. For snakes, we'll have our walking sticks, so we'll just flip 'em away..."

Molly and Kate burst out laughing.

Kate stopped long enough to say, "No problem. Just flip 'em away." As soon as the words cleared her lips, she started laughing again.

"Okay, before you two break your laughing box, there's one more thing. We'll clear out of the woods before dark," Ann said.

"And leave the woods all to the bear?" Kate said and started laughing anew.

"I'll continue when everyone's had their fun," Ann said.

Seeing that Ann was serious, Kate and Molly settled down.

"Good," Ann said. "Tomorrow, I'll shop for wearing apparel for the woods. Mother, I know your shoe size. Molly, what is yours?"

"Six," Molly said.

"Glove size?"

"Medium."

"Mother, medium for you?"

"Sure."

"Let's see. Mother's hat size would be extra-large," Ann said.

"You!" Kate shrieked, and then she grabbed a book and pretended to throw it.

"Oh, I'm sorry, Mother. I made a mistake. You're a medium," Ann said, and then she smiled.

"I knew you were just playing. Do you know why? Because you're my daughter, and we love each other."

Ann hugged her. "Can you be ready to leave at six o'clock day after tomorrow?" she whispered.

"Of course."

"Do we want to stop in Cookeville for breakfast?" Ann asked.

"I'd love it," Kate said.

"That okay with you, Molly?"

"I'm wids you, girl."

35

CHAPTER 3

"We're really doing this?" Kate said.

"Yes, three women on the way to catch Big Al," Ann said, and then she made a sound that was somewhere between a snarl and a laugh.

"Somehow, I find this a little comical," Molly said.

"It is a little odd, isn't it? On a different note, I bought three binoculars yesterday and a camera for you, Molly. That brings up a subject of the past, doesn't it?" Ann said.

"Does it ever. We're floating on a barge watching the scenery go by and nothing to record our big day," Molly recalled.

"Mother, she's talking about our riding a barge up the Cumberland River with no camera. That was in our past life."

They drove to Cookeville, had breakfast, then drove to Crab Orchard, passed Clay's house, and parked.

"There's Clay!" Molly said in a loud voice.

"Great! I'll be right back." Ann got out of the car and ran to meet Clay. Moments later, she returned. "Clay's allowing us to use that storage building anytime we want. We can change into our clothes that we're wearing into the woods."

"You could have introduced me," Kate said.

"Oh, hold on!" Ann said, and then she ran to Clay, and they both returned to the car. "Clay, I want you to meet Kate. Kate, meet Clay."

"Why, you look like sisters," Clay said in a tone of astonishment.

"We're closely related," Ann said.

"She's pulling your leg, Clay. I'm her mother."

"My golly! Nobody would believe that! Why, you look as young as she does."

"Ann, you found a great gentleman," Kate said. "And Clay, when you see my mother, Sara, you'll think we're all sisters. She looks as young as we do."

"Well, I never," Clay said. "By the way, about a quarter of a mile after you go into the woods, there seems to be a rattlesnake nest 'cause there's a snake sunning in the middle of the trail most of the time when you get to that spot. Be on the watch and be careful."

"What do we do if we see it?" Ann asked.

"Wait for it to leave, throw a rock at it, or if you have a long stick, just pick it up and flick it off the trail. Oh, I have a fourteen-foot-long strip of wood you can have. It's in the storage building. Hold on. I'll be back." Clay hurried away but returned immediately holding a one-inch by one-inch strip of wood. "This may help," he said.

"See, I told you," Ann said. "All we have to do is flick these things outta our way."

Kate and Molly looked at Ann with fearful expressions.

"Well, ladies, if you need anything anytime, let me know," Clay said, and then he walked away.

"That we will," Kate said, though Clay was out of earshot by the time she spoke. She looked at Ann and then at Molly. "Let's go get dressed."

They got several bags from the car and went to the storage building.

"He is really organized," Kate noted. "Look how everything is stacked just perfectly, and he uses pegboard for the small stuff. I'm impressed."

"His stone business is the same," Ann said. "Same color stones are on pallets, and the grounds are clean. We should look at our own businesses to see if we can do better with what we're doing."

"Okay, which one of these is mine?" Kate asked.

"Well, let's start with leather boots. Leather leggings will be next followed by leg snake protectors. You have a pellet pistol and a loaded nine-millimeter," Ann said. "Oh, I got a wristwatch for everyone. In case we don't have cell service, we'll still know what time it is.

"I just want to remind everyone that under no circumstances must you make any noise, especially like firing your weapon. Unless a bear has your arm or head in his or her mouth, please don't even think about firing your weapon.

"Also, everyone has binoculars."

"So, what's the plan?" Kate asked.

"First, we have to find the cabin. Once we find it, we watch it from a distance. Kate, you and Molly find a rock to perch on that's out of eyesight of Big Al. Just hang out there and watch the back of the cabin. I'll do the same except I'll watch the front of the cabin."

"Why perch on a rock?" Molly asked.

"So a snake doesn't bite your butt," Ann said.

Kate held her mouth to suppress a laugh.

Ann continued, "If Big Al is actually living in the cabin, he has to leave to use the bathroom, and he may even take a walk to relieve the boredom. If he has a weapon, he may go hunting, so be alert and be careful. Don't shoot him, though."

"I'm leathered up and ready," Kate said.

"Me too," Molly said.

"One more thing. When we start up the trail, use sign language. Don't talk," Ann said.

"What do we do if we haf to use the bafroom?" Molly asked.

"Go to the bottom of your rock but don't get off the rock," Ann said.

"Because?" Molly asked.

"Again, you don't want unwanted guests in the grass," Ann said.

"That's right. I keep forgettin' about gettin' bit in the butt," Molly said.

"Oh, here's a bottle of water for each of you and a package of crackers," Ann said.

"This is lunch?" Kate asked.

"I believe we'll be headed outta here around six tonight. If that holds true, I'll treat us to a late lunch in Cookeville. If you want to call it supper, we'll call it supper. Can we work with that?" Ann asked.

"Sure, we're big girls," Kate said. "Aren't we Molly?"

"Water and crackers will do the trick," Molly said, and then she smiled.

"Well, okay then. Are we ready?" Ann asked.

"Let's hit the road," Kate said.

They left the storage building, Ann picked up the long stick of wood, and then they began walking.

After about fifteen minutes, they walked up a small incline and started down the opposite side. Molly was leading the pack. Suddenly, she stopped in her tracks. Ann didn't stop and walked into her backside, nearly knocking her down. Molly panicked and grabbed furiously at Ann's arm, and then Ann saw the trail ahead of Molly. A coiled rattlesnake twitched its tail about eight feet in front of them, setting off its rattlers which caused an ominous sound that created fear in most people. Ann grabbed Molly's arm and jerked her backwards. Then she carefully eased the stick Clay had given her toward the snake which immediately struck it with its fangs. Appearing undisturbed, Ann eased the stick farther until the end began undercutting the snake's curled body. Apparently irritated, the snake uncurled and slithered into the thick undergrowth that bordered the trail.

Hurrying past the area where the snake had gone, Ann motioned for Kate and Molly to follow. They hesitated at first, but then they rushed to be with Ann, who looked at them and smiled. They continued walking.

The farther they walked, the more the ground became void of vegetation and underbrush. The denseness of the tree canopies prevented sunlight penetration and prevented growth. Also, the altitude grew, and the terrain became more rugged. Even with their youth, some of the climb was painful and nearly unbearable. Because of Molly's recent operation, several stops were necessary to rest.

On the last stop, Kate whispered to Ann, "I haven't seen any wild animals."

"Altitude's too high," Ann whispered.

The quietness of the mountains created an atmosphere of secrecy and mystery. The strange environment caused one to whisper in an unexplainable respect for the surroundings. Communication was almost in a reverent tone,

"Look! Look!" Ann said in a low but excitable voice while pointing toward an area where the mountain simply separated, creating a valley bordered by rocks heaped one onto another that rose at least one hundred feet. The scene was accentuated by a stream that poured water onto the top of the stack of rocks and then cascaded down, splashing harshly against the jagged assembly of rocks that Mother Nature had created.

Halfway down, the rocks stacked inward, allowing the water to fall freely. This waterfall dropped at least fifty feet to a large basin below. The basin always remained full, and the newly fallen water created an overflow that ran innocently off into a stream that flowed down the mountain.

Kate's eyes enlarged as she stared at the display that had taken thousands of years of construction by Mother Nature. She looked at Ann, held out her hands, and whispered, "It's beautiful."

"Why don't I just wait for you here?" Molly said.

"It's too dangerous," Ann said, using a low voice. "Not only do we have to worry about animals, but we have to worry about Big Al. We can wait here as long as you need, though."

"No, no, I'm okay. I just thought I was being a drag," Molly said.

"You have never been a drag and never will be," Ann said.

"Let's go," Molly said.

They continued walking, and there was a noticeable change in everyone's attitude. They seemed to discover the beauty of the mountain.

Trees seemed to rise to the sky providing a canopy that painted the area beneath them a light gray in color. One could look in every direction and see the same gray color with tree trunks reaching for the sky. Dead logs lay here and there that helped create a scene of an ageless forest unconquered by man or beast.

Another distinctive feature was the quietness. There were no birds, and there were no animals. When the wind blew, it simply rattled the tops of the trees, and the forest floor remained quiet.

Ann stopped and searched the area with binoculars. They were far in the mountains, and it seemed as if they were looking for something that didn't exist. After a few moments, they continued walking. The direction they were walking was parallel with the crest of the mountain range which was around two hundred feet above them.

Suddenly something touched Ann's arm, and she jerked and looked behind her. Kate was close to her and pointed to her right.

Ann looked in the direction Kate was pointing and saw a well-worn trail that went to a clump of trees and disappeared. Ann pointed at herself and then pointed at the clump of trees. She pointed at Kate and at the ground.

Kate nodded that she understood she was to remain there.

Ann pulled her weapon and walked slowly to the clump of trees. The trail made a semi-circle around the trees and stretched straight up the mountainside. Replacing the weapon in its holster, she followed the trail with her binoculars. The dim light impaired her vision, but then a very dull image of a cabin appeared. The picture was so unexpected and prominent that she jerked the binoculars hard against her face, causing the area around her eyes to hurt.

Cautiously retracing her steps down the mountainside, she returned to meet Kate. "There's a cabin about three hundred feet beyond that clump of trees," she whispered, "and there's a tall stack of rocks to the left of it. Do you think you and Molly can get to the rocks without being seen?"

"Of course. What's the plan?"

"I'm going to the right. We're going to watch the cabin until five o'clock. That'll give us an hour and a half to get outta here. The bad thing is we have no communication, so if you have a real big problem, fire your weapon and I'll do the same."

Kate and Molly went to the left of the trail. Ann watched until they appeared as little specks among the trees, and then she started up the mountain to the right of the trail.

I have so much to watch, she thought. *I have to watch the ground for snakes; I have to watch the entire area for the unknown; I have to watch for Big Al.* She remembered walking through the woods north of Knoxville to perform a sniper job. Those woods were close, and the visibility was not good. These woods were wide open with tree trunks reaching to the sky, but there were clumps of dead leaves or rotting tree trunks that were plentiful along the forest floor, providing the ideal nests for snakes, spiders, and other varmints. She tried to avoid those areas.

As she walked, leaves rustled, creating within her a mental insecurity with every step. Seeing a barren spot, she stopped and looked through the binoculars. Jerking back, she saw the cabin looming so near on the lenses that she immediately lowered the binoculars to assure herself she was not standing on the cabin doorstep. Backing up hurriedly, she realized that the cabin was not as far from the clump of trees as she once thought. The realization reverberated in her head.

Now the critical and immediate problem was to find a safe place that could be used for surveillance. She had hoped for a large rock that could be used for a perch, but there wasn't anything that she could see that would fit her plan. Thinking she had to improvise, she suddenly did a double take. A giant tree branch had split off from the mother tree about eight feet from the ground and was still attached. Its upper branches provided a wedge with the ground. *It's perfect,* Ann thought. *I'll be off the ground, and I don't have to worry about a snake. It's almost a straight chair. I can sit on the broken branch and let my back rest on the main tree trunk.*

She stepped on the broken branch that lay gouged into the ground and then walked upwards toward the trunk of the tree. When she was about four feet off the ground, the incline became too great, so she bent down and crawled the remaining distance. When she reached the split from the main trunk, she smiled. *I can see the whole world,* she thought. *How lucky can one be!* Looking through the binoculars, she was even more amazed. Both the front and back of the cabin flashed before her eyes as if she were standing just outside the walls.

She thought of Kate and Molly. *I hope they have been so lucky.*

Okay, I can't and don't want to hold these binoculars for seven hours, so I'll put this leg against that branch and the other leg against the other branch, and then I'll just balance my elbows on my knees and watch that cabin until Big Al comes out.

Suddenly the leaves rustled beneath her which startled her. Pulling the nine-millimeter from its holster, she peered over the edge of the branch. *A dog! Big Al's dog? Skinny little thing. That's no dog, silly,* she thought. *Dogs don't have pointed ears and thin noses. It's a red fox! What're you doing out here?*

Reminding herself she was on surveillance; she looked through the binoculars. *Big Al!! It's Big Al,* she thought. *I could pop him right now, but that's too good for him.* She had something else in mind. It was 10:30 a.m. and the first sighting. She made a mental note of it.

She watched him stroll leisurely to the clump of trees and then return to the cabin. *He didn't use the restroom, so this must have been a stretch-my-legs break,* she thought.

Continuing to watch through the day, Big Al took a stretch-my-legs break close to 1:30, a restroom run near 2:30, and a final stretch-my-legs break at 4:30.

At 5:30 Ann slid off the limb and walked hurriedly to the trail below the clump of trees. A few moments later, Kate and Molly met her.

"Everything okay?" Ann asked.

"It worked out really good," Kate said. "We recorded Big Al four times, and Molly killed a snake that crawled up the rock to be with us."

"Yuk!" Ann said. "Well, I saw the same thing as you and Molly except for the snake. Are we ready to get off this mountain?"

"It can't be quick enough," Kate said.

"We have some Suzuki King Quad's at the produce company," Ann said. "They don't make a lotta noise, and the guys at the shop rigged them to carry a passenger. I'll ask Clay if we can park three of them at his place."

"Now you're talking," Kate said.

"Aren't they called ATVs?" Molly said.

"They are," Ann said. "That's what we'll call 'em. Let's set up this same surveillance two more times to see if Big Al repeats his strolls in the woods at the same times every day," Ann said.

"Sounds good," Kate said.

They walked off the mountain, and then Ann talked to Clay who gave his permission to park the four-wheelers and even volunteered to secure them with chain and lock when they were not in use.

After talking with Clay, Ann told Kate and Molly that she would have her manager, Dave, get two four-wheelers ready for tomorrow. They would use the produce company's pickup truck and trailer to haul them.

"We're through here. Let's go home," Kate said.

"I agree," Ann said, and then they got into the car, and Ann drove them back to Nashville.

The next two days, they duplicated what they had done on the first day. A big difference, though, was they rode four-wheelers close to the trail that led to Big Al's cabin. They used the same observation areas; they watched the cabin until 5:00; they recorded the times Big Al left the cabin, which were the same times for all three days. He definitely was a creature of habit.

When they left Crab Orchard on the third day, they drove to Kate's house for a meeting. Sara had prepared deli sandwiches and home fries for everyone. They ate first, and then Sara called the meeting to begin.

Kate and Molly elected Ann to speak of their findings in Crab Orchard.

"Kate and Molly observed Big Al's cabin for the last three days on the left side of the cabin, and I observed the cabin on the right side," Ann said. "We both recorded that Big Al left the cabin four times each day and at practically the same times each day. His last time each day was 4:30. I could have easily popped him on any of the times he left the cabin on any day, but I propose something different. Big Al is an evil man, and evil men deserve that evil be turned on them."

"What do you propose, Ann?" Sara asked.

"I propose we remove Big Al by using a camouflaged pit that contains punji sticks."

"What's that?" Cynthia asked.

"It's a pit with sharpened stakes planted at the bottom of the pit," Ann said.

"That seems really complicated," Sara said.

"Kate and Molly, if I were digging the pit, I would dig it on the trail just before the turn at the clump of trees. The big problem is how to dig it without making noise, how to get it done in one night, and what to do with the dirt."

"Ann, there's a wide sink hole about a hundred feet from the clump of trees. We passed it when we left the clump of trees for our stakeout," Kate said.

"I got friends, and we can get the pit dug without noise," Molly said.

Ann's eyes lit up. "All right!" she said loudly. "Well then, there are the stakes. How do we get the stakes in the bottom of the pit?"

"Use four by fours, drill holes in them, and then anchor twelve-inch stakes in the holes," Molly said.

"Girl, you are full of surprises! You need a contractor's license," Ann said. "How did you learn all this stuff?"

"Tent City. They taught me how to survive," Molly said.

Everyone laughed.

"Make the four by fours seven feet long an' haf at least ten of them," Molly said. "In each one, drill a hole four inches from the end an' insert a twelve-inch stake with the sharp end down so that it can be driven into the ground to secure the four by four. Then take a hand-held saw and sharpen the end that sticks up."

"So, you will get the pit dug?" Ann asked.

"Yeah, I will," Molly said.

"Can you get the stakes prepared?" Ann asked.

"Yeah."

"So, how do we get Big Al and the pit to meet?" Sara asked.

"We get two pieces of plywood, cut handholes in one side of each of the pieces, and then we place the plywood over the pit," Ann said. "The plywood will be wide enough so that there will be a twelve-inch lip on each side that rests on the shoulder of the pit. The handholes will be on the outer side of the trail. We cover the plywood with dry leaves to camouflage it."

"Molly, can you get the plywood delivered?"

"No problem."

"You'll need some light…"

"Got it. Big Al will never see the light."

"I still haven't heard how we get Big Al and the pit to meet," Sara said.

"I dress in short red shorts and appear on the trail below the cabin at four-twenty-five," Ann explained. "Big Al will see me and approach me. I start running and Big Al starts running. I run past the clump of trees and across the plywood. Sara is on one side of the trail, and Kate is on the other side. They have their hands through the handholes in the plywood. As soon as I clear the plywood, Sara and Kate pull the plywood away from the pit, and Big Al goes headfirst and belly first into the pit." She looked at everyone and waited. Then she said, "Well?"

"What if the plywood breaks when you run over it?" Cynthia asked in a squeaky voice.

"It wouldn't dare," Ann said.

"When do we start?" Sara asked.

"Molly, how soon can you be ready?" Ann asked.

"Day after tomorrow night," Molly said.

"So, the day after tomorrow night will be get-the-pit-ready night. Then the big chase will be at four thirty the next day," Ann said. "Sara and Kate, can you be on the mountain day after tomorrow night?"

"Count me in," Sara said.

"Wouldn't miss it for the world," Kate said.

Ann rubbed her hands together. "I just love it when a complex puzzle goes together. I'll rent a block of rooms at a hotel in Crossville in case anyone wants to get some sleep. The police department will pick up the tab so we won't be out any money."

Cynthia looked at Kate and a wide smile blossomed on her face. "Ain't she smart? She's the smartest person I've ever seen," Cynthia said, looking at Ann.

"Don't blow her up too much, Cynthia. Her head might explode," Kate said.

Cynthia stared at Kate with an are-you-serious? look for a few moments, and then she burst out laughing. She pointed a finger at Kate and said, "You! You!" The statement was Cynthia's way of telling Kate she should recognize Ann's intelligence.

CHAPTER 4

"This is a beautiful part of our state," Sara said.

"It's beautiful twelve hundred feet up," Kate said, "and today you get to see it."

"At least we have the four-wheelers," Ann said. "We should be just below the clump of trees by a quarter of four. If it works out, I'm going to see if Big Al sticks to his agenda and takes the four-thirty walk. He made a U-turn about a hundred feet from the clump of trees the three days we saw him. I would like to know if he ever deviates from that routine."

"Do you want me to go with you?" Kate said.

"No, I'll be okay, and we can't leave Sara all alone. A bear may get 'er."

"A bear would run from me," Sara said.

"Run with you hanging outta its mouth," Kate said.

They all laughed.

"We told you about Clay's house, Sara. We're here. We'll put on our wild animal duds here. I'll get yours, Sara. They're in the trunk," Ann said. They put on their protective gear and rode the four-wheelers about a hundred feet short of the clump of trees.

Ann got off and grabbed her binoculars. "I'll be back shortly," she said.

"Be careful," Sara said.

"I will." She hurried up the same way she had done for three consecutive days. When she reached the broken tree, she whispered, "I'm back, old friend. You haven't changed at all." She climbed and crawled just as she had the last three times until she reached the main trunk, and then she waited.

A hawk flew over and whistled "Kee-eee, kee-eee," and then it disappeared in the tops of the trees. She had heard the sound many times and believed the hawk had finished its day and was announcing it was home.

Oh, oh, four thirty. There he comes, she thought. She watched as he walked down the trail, made a U-turn in precisely the same spot that he did the other three days, and then he returned to the cabin.

She scooted down the tree limb and returned to the clump of trees. "Whoa," she said. A black piece of material resembling a king-size blanket was stretched across the trail.

Circumventing the material by walking in a wide semicircle, she looked up and uttered a second "Whoa." She looked and blinked and then looked again. She couldn't believe the activity in front of her. Ten very thin men scurried here and there as if they were totally out of control.

"Whatta ya think?"

Ann turned quickly to see Molly. "Whatta ya think? I mean, whatta I think? It looks like a hustling, bustling menagerie."

"These guys are going to dig the pit. They don't have any idea why or what for. As soon as they get done, they're gone."

"Well, I can think of a thousand questions, but the first one is what are they going to do with the dirt? It just can't be piled up for Big Al to see."

"That's well under control. Follow me."

Ann followed Molly a few feet from the clump of trees. An area had been cleared, and a tarp was spread out on the ground. It held stacks of equipment. She touched Molly's arm. Her emerald-green eyes were ordinarily large and sparkled even in the dim light. "I know what those are. We have them at the produce company. They're mobile conveyor belts!"

"You won the prize, girl! That's exactly what they are."

"So, tell me what's going to happen."

"The guys all work in construction. As soon as they get their measurements straight, they're going to start digging. They'll set up the conveyors, and they'll take the dirt to the sinkhole. We haf plastic containers to hold the dirt. One guy will be at the sinkhole to empty the dirt, and another guy will watch the dirt movement on the conveyor. The black cloth is to block some sound plus block any light that escapes from the pit. When it gets dark, they will use lights with hoods which will stop the light being seen up the trail.

"We haf heavy cloth to go on the rollers, so there'll be no sound when we move the dirt to the sinkhole. Do you want to see the four by fours?"

"Absolutely."

They walked to an area just beyond the conveyors. Two wooden crates held five four by fours each. There were eight twelve-inch stakes that were twelve inches apart in each four by four. On each end an inverted stake was incorporated into the four by four and looked to be the same length as the other stakes.

"When we're ready, two of the guys will be lowered into the pit. Then the four by fours will be lowered. The guys will drive the end stakes into the ground to anchor the four by fours. There'll be coverage for every two inches of the pit. In other words, there'll only be two inches of open space between the four by fours.

"Now there's a surprise! We haf three concrete blocks that're twelve inches by six inches. Each one of them haf three twelve-inch pieces of rebar concreted into them."

"Molly, Molly, Molly, what can I say? You are the best. I absolutely am in awe at what you've done. Do you realize we're undertaking a major project, and you've contributed the whole thing?"

"I'm happy to help," Molly said.

"Have Sara and Kate seen all this?"

"Oh, yeah. I gave 'em the two-dollar tour, and they're impressed... really impressed!"

"Oh my! I just had a frightening thought. We don't have anyone watching the trail to make sure Big Al doesn't creep up on us."

"I can watch," Molly said.

"You're too important; you need to stay here to oversee the project. I'll watch but promise me that you'll let me know if there's a problem."

"Of course," Molly said.

Ann walked around the black blanket that was strung across the trail, leaned against a tree, and watched the trail.

After a short time, Kate came to meet her. "It's my watch," she said. "You need to see those guys work! It's unbelievable. They're going to be finished by nine o'clock."

"Whoa! So, you don't mind watching for a few minutes?" Ann said.

"I'll stay until dark. By that time, they should be nearly finished," Kate said.

"You know, rather than drag this out all the way to tomorrow afternoon, why don't we just do our thing on his first walk tomorrow morning?" Ann said.

"I agree. Let's ask Sara," Kate said.

"I'll get her," Ann said, and then she went around the curtain and met Sara. "Can you break away for a short meeting?"

"Sure. What's up?"

"Let's go around the curtain," Ann said.

Sara followed Ann, and they met Kate.

"You go, Kate," Ann said.

"I was telling Ann that the guys are working so fast that they probably will finish by nine o'clock. Ann suggested we go ahead with the project at ten-thirty tomorrow morning."

"That's his first walk?" Sara asked.

"As far as we know," Ann said.

"Well, I'm for it," Sara said. "Let's just do it and get off the mountain. I think we should add a feature to the pit, though."

"What's that?" Kate asked.

"I think we should place a piece of wood across the pit to support the pieces of plywood when Ann runs across."

"Sara, you don't think the plywood will hold?" Ann said.

"I just don't want the plywood to slide off the side or break and then see you hanging on a stake in the pit."

"Uhh. Since you put it that way, I'm in. Let's find a piece of wood to go across the pit. As soon as I get across, how do we get the wood off the pit? It'll be hard to get to because the plywood will be in the way. We don't want to break Big Al's fall for sure."

"We'll make the piece of wood longer than the plywood, so it sticks out. When I pull my piece of plywood off the pit, I'll slide the piece of wood to one side, so it won't interfere with Big Al," Kate said.

"Sounds good," Ann said. "Whatta you think, Sara?"

"I believe it'll work. Let's do at least two dry runs before we do the real thing," Sara said.

"Two it is," Ann said. "That okay with you, Kate?"

"I concur," Kate said.

"Any other thing we need to discuss?" Sara asked.

"Not for me," Kate said.

"Me three," Ann said. "I'll relieve you a little later, Kate."

"I'll be here," Kate said.

Ann and Sara returned to the side where the pit was being dug. Eight men were digging in teams of two.

"Whatta you think?" Molly said.

"They are like a machine," Ann said. "One man on each team fills the plastic tub with dirt, the second man immediately gives him an empty tub, and then the second man puts the full tub on the conveyor belt. Filled tubs are going on the conveyor belt as if they were coming off an assembly line. Amazing!"

"And they swap out jobs about every thirty minutes," Molly said.

"The whole project is quite impressive," Sara said. "Since it will be finished so quickly, and after the men leave, what do you say we put the plywood over the pit, cover the plywood with dried leaves, and then go to the hotel for a good night's sleep?" Sara said.

"Sounds great. The thing that concerns me, though, is what if Big Al takes a walk at seven in the morning and strolls down and sees the pit?" Ann said.

"What if we just be here at six-thirty in the morning?" Sara suggested.

"We?" Ann said.

"We. Your good-looking grandmother and your beautiful mother," Sara said.

Ann looked at her and burst out laughing.

Sara put her finger to her lips and said, "Shhh. Big Al may hear you."

"Okay. Okay. I'm under control. I like your plan. We'll do it as long as my beautiful mother agrees," Ann said.

Sara's cheeks moved to form a smile, but she pulled back and said, "Let's check with her."

"I'll be back," Ann said, and then she went around the curtain and met Kate.

"Grandmother Sara suggested we go to the hotel after the pit is finished and come back tomorrow morning by six-thirty. That okay with you?"

"I'm for that. A nice shower and a good meal or even a mediocre meal would be great," Kate said.

"Okay, I'll stand watch. Give me a soft yell when we're ready to go." Ann leaned against the tree she had used on her first watch.

Dusk came, and Ann felt a little anxious. *How much longer?* she thought.

"You look like you're about to run away, girl," Molly said.

"Whoa! I didn't see you come around the curtain," Ann said.

"I didn't mean to startle you," Molly said. "I just come to tell you that they finished. The four by fours are in the pit, and the plywood's over the pit. The guys are halfway down the mountain by now."

"Well, let's go, girl," Ann said. "We're going to the hotel and get some sleep. Be back here at six-thirty tomorrow morning."

Everyone left the mountain, drove to Crossville, had a snack, and went to bed.

The next morning, they returned to the mountain and started up in the ATVs. When they had driven several hundred feet and were in an area with heavy brush, several wild hogs crashed into Kate's and Sara's ATVs, causing Kate to perilously lose control. The hogs were black in color and moved close to the ground. They were short and stout and moved with irregular bursts of speed. They appeared intent on removing anything in their woods.

A constant mixture of grunting, snorting, and shrill sounds created an even more grizzly scene.

Seeing their predicament, Ann turned her four-wheeler so that it aimed directly at the hogs, and it struck one directly in the mid-section. The hog squealed and acted as if it would attack Ann's four-wheeler, but it apparently had a change of mind and ran into the brush. The remaining hogs slammed into Kate's ATV so hard that it would have turned over except for Ann's ATV providing a buffer for it.

Additional hogs joined the group and seemed intent on turning over Kate's ATV. Ann continually maneuvered her ATV to help Kate, but the hogs were beginning to win the battle. The continuous grunting and snorting were also beginning to take their toll.

Suddenly, Molly and Cynthia drove up. Seeing what was happening, Molly gunned her ATV and rammed the hogs.

Seeing Molly, Ann immediately vowed to change the momentum. She gunned her vehicle and pushed two hogs to the ground, and then she ran over them. The impact lifted her vehicle high above the ground then dropped it abruptly.

Kate joined the assault. Her vehicle surged ahead, hitting two of the hogs in the rear end. The jolt shoved them several feet away from the melee, and then they split and ran into the brush.

Ann ran through the middle of another group, and then Molly pulled up beside Ann and together they pushed the hogs off the trail.

Looking at Kate and then Molly, Ann held up her hand and motioned for them to follow her. They immediately fell in line and started up the mountain. Only a few minutes later, they arrived at the clump of trees, and then they got off their vehicles.

"Hogs! Bunch of hogs!" Ann hissed. "They threw us off our schedule! Now we don't know if Big Al took an early walk!"

"We'll just have to go with his ten-thirty walk," Kate said. "We need to do two or three dry runs for our project."

"Before I run across a pit that's full of sharp stakes, I'm going to inspect it," Ann said.

Kate laughed. "You might try tiptoeing across it first," she said.

"I'm going to inspect it ten times before I set a toe on it," Ann said.

"Let's look," Kate said.

They walked to the pit and scraped the brush and leaves off the plywood. Ann carefully inspected the sides to assure herself that the sides fit smugly, and the plywood wouldn't bow and dump her into the pit.

"I'll walk across," Sara said.

"Sara, you're the plywood operator. I'll walk across, and then let's try a dry run," Ann said.

"Sounds good," Sara said.

Ann exhaled loudly and then put one foot on the plywood. Staying very close to the side of the pit, she took another step. Watching the ends of the plywood to make sure they didn't bend with her weight, she ventured farther along the plywood. When she got to the middle, the wood bowed slightly, and she stopped and stood still for a few moments. Becoming more comfortable and believing the wood had bowed to its greatest extent, she ventured farther. When she was close to two-thirds across, she took a large lunge, hit the wood with one foot, and landed on solid ground with the other.

Sara and Kate stood together, and each raised a thumb to congratulate her.

Ann smiled, walked around the pit to the side where she began her walk, and then she ran lightly across the wood to the other side.

"Okay, I'm going to take another run a little faster, and then one at full speed. Sara and Kate, when I make the full-speed run, please pull the plywood back," Ann said. As she had stated, she made the runs, and the plywood slid freely and easily.

The tracks where the wood rested had been excavated four inches below the surface of the earth and were four inches wide. A four-inch-wide aluminum strip had been placed on the earthen track and secured to the track by Molly's workers. The result was the tracks were slick as glass, and it took little effort to scoot the plywood away from the pit.

"Okay, let's put the plywood back in place and please, please make sure it's anchored in against the track walls," Ann said.

Sara and Kate slid their pieces back so they were snug inside the tracks and covered the pit just as snuggly.

Ann inspected the wood, and then she circled the pit to make sure the sides of the wood were in place.

"I'm going full speed this time," Ann said. "Mother, I'll be running on your side as close to the apron as possible. If something goes wrong at least I'll have a chance to grab the side of the pit. If I'm going fast, I should only hit the wood two times. As soon as I clear the wood, jerk the wood. This is going to be a real-life dress rehearsal."

"I'll be with you in spirit every second, honey," Kate said.

"Let's do it," Ann said as she marched several feet away from the pit. "Ready?"

"We're ready," Kate said.

Ann visibly took a deep breath and started running. After four steps, she was running full speed. Her right foot hit the board about two feet from the beginning of the pit, and then her left foot landed a short distance from the opposite side. Her right leg appeared as a flash as it lifted and moved ahead, and then her foot landed on the earth as smoothly and quietly as a highly talented athlete. She looked back and smiled.

Just as she cleared the pit, Sara and Kate pulled the wood away from the pit.

Ann walked around the pit. "Let's do it one more time," she said.

Sara and Kate slid their pieces of wood over the pit.

"Please look it over," Sara said.

Ann inspected the placement of the wood and said, "Looks good. Let's do it." Walking a short distance, she turned to make her run, then sped toward the pit. This time she ran to her left and to Sara's side. It took only two steps to clear the pit. If a stopwatch had been used to time clearance of the wood, it would have barely started to time Ann's speed.

Sara and Kate pulled the wood to expose the pit as soon as Ann's feet hit the earth.

Ann walked back to Sara's side and asked Kate to join them. When Kate joined them, Ann said, "Running to my left doesn't feel natural. It feels like I'm running against the grain. It feels weird, so I'll be running to your side, Mother. Do you understand, Grandmother?"

"Of course I do, honey. It is awkward running to one's left."

"Good! It's show time! I'm going over behind that tree to change clothes. I'll be back in a few." She picked up a bag she had brought up the mountain and walked to a tree with a trunk so large that it would take the arms of two men to wrap around it.

A few minutes later, she returned dressed in red short shorts, a white silk blouse tied at the bottom to show her midriff, and her red hair tied in a bouncy ponytail.

Molly hurried to join the group. "Whoa! Miss Holly…wood!" she said.

"Honey, you need to be on the cover of a glamour magazine. You would grace it with your presence," Kate said, her face beaming with admiration.

"You sure are pretty," Sara said. "I agree with everything that's been said and even more. You be careful."

Ann smiled. "It's time," she said. "I want to check the wood, and then I'll walk up the path toward the cabin. Will all of you cover the wood with leaves?"

"We will," Kate said. "Please be careful."

"I will," Ann said. She inspected the wood placement, stood back and looked at it for a few moments, and then she started up the trail.

It was twenty after ten.

Ann walked slowly. Occasionally, she leaned over and looked at a sapling that was poking its head through the dirt. The sun lit up a small spot in front of her. It was a rarity for this part of the mountain. There was an open spot in the canopy above her, and the sun took full advantage of it by slipping bright rays of sun down to the earth.

Ann very carefully stuck one foot into the light. It was a whimsical thing to do, but she also wanted to see what would happen.

Suddenly, she heard a noise. Looking up quickly at the cabin, she saw a large man emerge from the doorway. He was absolutely three men packed into one, and there was no flab on his body. Ann thought he resembled a giant that Hollywood invented and one that caused the earth to moan and tremble when he took a step. He could turn over a medium-size van with no help while using only a little effort. He was Big Al.

Ann took a step toward him. She felt tiny. He didn't move, so she took another. Her eyes were fixated on his, and she used body language to tease him. She started to step again, but he stepped toward her. Almost instantly, she began backing up, but he continued toward her, so she began to run. Looking back, she was shocked to see that he was moving much faster. His stride was so long that he covered as much space in one stride as she did in three steps. Still looking back, she ran faster. He picked up speed, causing her to run even faster.

Glancing quickly toward the clump of trees, Ann believed she was less than a hundred feet from the turn at the trees and the pit just beyond. Looking back at Big Al, her heart instantly beat faster. He was much closer than just seconds ago. A thought whizzed through her head that she was practically at top speed. With Big Al's long stride, there was a chance that he could catch her before she got to the pit. *Run faster!* she thought. *Run faster!* She heard his feet pound on the ground. He was like something mechanical. Only a few more inches and his arms could entrap her like a giant octopus.

Run! Run! Run!

Suddenly, she felt her right foot hit the wood covering the pit, then the left foot. In a flash, she cleared the wood, ran a couple of steps, and stopped. Looking back, she saw that Sara and Kate had pulled the wood away from the top of the pit to expose it. Then she choked and her heart seemingly stopped. Big Al had stopped just short of the pit! He just stood there like a massive tree trunk.

Ann's heart beat even faster. *What now?* She looked toward Kate then Sara. They looked back at her with drawn faces. A thousand thoughts raced through her head. Someone has to shoot him, but she didn't have a weapon. Did Sara or Kate have a weapon?

Suddenly, Big Al moved forward a little more. All at once his body bent forward, then teetered back and forth until the movement robbed his stability, and then he tumbled into the pit. "Ohhh!" he yelled in a deep voice so loud that it traveled throughout the woods. He yelled again, but the sound of his voice was weaker. It changed to a moaning sound. Then it was quiet.

Ann couldn't believe her eyes. Was she dreaming or hoping for the best? She shook her head and looked again. "Cynthia?" she uttered.

Cynthia stood where Big Al had stood only seconds ago.

Ann hurried to be with her. "Cynthia," she said again.

"I shoved him," Cynthia said, her voice low and humble-sounding.

Ann looked down into the pit. Big Al lay in a prone position. Three stakes had impaled his body. Other stakes could be seen penetrating his body, but they did not protrude as the first three.

She looked at Cynthia and then put her arm around her. "You sure did," she said.

Kate and Sara rushed to join them.

"Cynthia, are you okay?" Sara asked.

"Yes, ma'am. I thought I needed to help."

"And help you did. You were a savior, Cynthia. You saved this entire project."

"I did?"

"Yes, honey, you did," Sara said, and then she looked into the pit and focused her attention on Big Al. "You'll never kill anyone else; you'll never rape anyone else; you'll never rob anyone of their freedom again. It was a mistake for you to be on this earth. You were a worthless piece of trash."

Kate stepped alongside Sara and looked down at Big Al. "We let you off too easy. You deserved a much worse ending than this, but you're gone. You were a cancer to civilization."

Molly joined them. "He's gone," she said.

"Much too easy," Kate said. "Mother, I'll take a picture for the chief. That'll confirm this piece of trash has been apprehended."

"And he can come and pull the trash outta the hole," Sara said.

"Whatta you say we get our gear and get off this mountain?" Ann said.

A unanimous chorus of yesses followed.

CHAPTER 5

A week passed after Big Al's demise on the mountain. The Patterson family had voted to take a week off to catch up on personal matters. They believed apprehending Pinkie would take a longer investigation period than that of Big Al, so the break would provide some benefit to everyone.

After the week's end, Sara called a meeting to be held at Kate's house. She had set the meeting for seven o'clock, but she arrived twenty minutes early.

'Hi, Mother, or is it Sara?"

"Is it possible I was a foolish woman? The names are confusing, aren't they?" Sara said.

"I think just call you Mother and Ann call me Mother," Kate said.

"Agreed."

"Agreed. Okay, what is the meeting about?"

"I would like to talk about Molly's education and then how we go about apprehending Pinkie."

"Great. Oh, there's Ann and her crew," Kate said, and then she opened the door, and Ann, Molly, and Cynthia went inside.

"Don't tell me our vacation is over," Ann said.

Sara smiled. "I haven't seen any of you for a whole week. I thought we'd all get together and visit."

"Sara…"

"It's Grandmother, dear granddaughter. My suggestion about using formal names was foolish. That's your mother," Sara said, pointing toward Kate, "and I'm your grandmother. Isn't that wonderful?"

"Whoa! I do believe I'm awakening from a bad dream," Ann said. "Mother, did you hear what she just said?"

"Miracles never stop in this family," Kate said.

Molly and Cynthia giggled.

"I do have some little items to discuss," Sara said. "Does anyone want a drink before we start?"

"I'll get 'em," Ann said. "Molly, do you want the usual?"

"Please."

"Cynthia, do you want mother's famous tea?"

Cynthia hesitated for a moment.

Ann laughed. "It's okay. You're part of the family."

"Okay," Cynthia said.

Ann went to the kitchen and returned with a tray of drinks and chips. "Dig in," she said.

Everyone got their drink and chips then took their seats.

"I have an announcement," Sara said. "We got our first paycheck. It was two hundred thousand, but I couldn't persuade the tightwad chief to cover all our out-of-pocket expenses. The conveyors were quite expensive. After we paid everything that we had to pay, we have one hundred eighty-thousand left. So, I suggest fifty goes to me, fifty to Kate, and fifty to Ann. That leaves thirty to be split between Molly and Cynthia."

Molly gasped.

"Grandmother," Ann said, "I made a lotta money in recent weeks. It's embarrassing to think about it, so I'm splitting my share between Molly and Cynthia. That'll give Molly a starter fund for school and a down payment for a car for Cynthia."

Molly slumped in her chair. "Wha…." she muttered.

Cynthia leaned forward in her chair. Her eyes had grown extraordinarily large, but they looked ahead with a blank stare. "Uh, uh, you're…you're givin' your money to me?" she said, her words coming slow and measured.

"I am," Ann said.

"I'm gettin' a car?"

"Well, not immediately, but you're getting a car for sure."

Cynthia jumped from her chair and embraced Ann. "I love you," she said.

Ann pulled back and appeared shocked. "If a car makes you that happy, I'll get you a big rig," Ann said.

Everyone laughed.

"I wuz just happy," Cynthia said. "I never had a family that made me so happy."

"Well, just count on a lifetime of happiness," Ann said.

"All right, ladies. Another item on our agenda is to have Molly pass the GED as soon as possible. I've arranged for Molly to take a four-week study course that has an excellent track record. Molly, are you ready to get smarter?"

"Ready and willing. Can I help you track down Pinkie before I start?"

"You start the course in two weeks, so you can look for Pinkie for two weeks.

"Ann, do you have any thoughts about apprehending Pinkie?"

"Grandmother, I do. Molly and I will concentrate on the uncle's house…sleep during the day and watch the house at night. We'll be on stakeout twenty-four, seven though."

"Sounds good," Sara said. "Let's you, me, and Kate meet in the kitchen."

Once they were in the kitchen, everyone was silent. It was like a serious ritual that the three of them valued highly and respected.

"Ladies, here are your marbles," Sara said, and then she gave one black and one white to each of them. "Ann, do you want to start the vote?"

"Yes." She went to the kitchen counter and dropped a marble into the cup that was used for the voting process.

Kate followed Ann, and then Sara went to the counter and dropped a marble into the cup. She immediately emptied the cup, observed the marbles that had been used to vote, and returned to meet with Kate and Ann.

"I have the results of our voting," Sara said. "There are two black and one white. That, of course, means that the emphasis on the apprehension of Pinkie is that he is to perish. However, if his behavior convinces the apprehender that he has remorse and he has left his criminal life behind him, and he has potential of becoming a positive force in society, then he can be saved."

"Grandmother, you have such a grasp of the English language. You could actually be an English professor," Ann said.

"Kate, your daughter has finally realized what an intellectual her grandmother is. Can you believe how many years it has taken for her to realize it?"

Everyone laughed.

"Molly and I will go to Triune tomorrow," Ann volunteered. "We'll make it a point to be there before five just in case someone comes home around five o'clock. We'll stay all night the first night to see if there's any coming or going."

"Honey, do you want to take something to keep you awake?" Kate asked.

"No, Mother, thank you for being so thoughtful and motherly. What we'll do is to call you if we start nodding," Ann said.

"Mother," Kate said, turning to Sara, "was I ever as sassy a daughter as my daughter is with me?"

"Honey, all young women are sassy…for a few years anyway. It passes."

Cynthia giggled.

"Okay, all you great oracles can have all the fun you want, but Molly and I are going to nail Pinkie," Ann said.

Sara and Kate jumped from their chairs and hugged Ann and Molly.

"We love both of you," they said simultaneously.

"Both of you better take a jacket, because it's supposed to be chilly tomorrow, and especially at night," Kate said.

CHAPTER 6

Only a week had passed since Labor Day, but it seemed like someone had pulled a switch and turned summer into fall.

"Are we goin' to get cold tonight?" Molly asked.

"Well, you might, but I brought a coat," Ann said. "When we were all together last night, Mother told us it might be chilly today."

Molly was silent.

Ann laughed. "I was just joshin' with you, girl. I have a coat for you on the back seat."

"Girl, you are just full of it. I never want to run into you on Halloween."

Ann laughed again. "Boo!" she said in a loud, deep voice.

Molly laughed. "Okay, I'll change th' subject. When will th' leaves start changing?"

"They've started. You just haven't noticed. It's still beautiful along here, don't you think?" Ann said.

"It is. Do you kno' I haf never been this way?"

"When we finish these gigs, you're going to be a world traveler. I promise you. Besides, you need to know about various places when you become a high-falutin' attorney."

"I took a barge ride once. Does that count?" Molly said.

"You used one of your nine lives on that ride, girl," Ann said, remembering when they took a barge ride just for fun and to break the monotony of living on the bank of the Cumberland River. "I thought you were a dead barge passenger that I let go for a swim while thinking subconsciously that it was going to be very difficult to get you back on the barge," Ann said.

"Well, you got me back on the barge…you and that big hunk on the dock," Molly said, referring to the dockworker that pulled her out of the water and back onto the barge.

"Yeah, he's on our 'good contact' list. Hey! We're in Triune," Ann said.

"And it's still light," Molly said.

"That'll give us time to find a place to hang out. I'm going to stop and put the uncle's address in my phone."

"How does she do that?" Molly asked.

"She who?" Ann said.

"The lady in the telephone. How does she kno' where to go?" Molly said.

"Look at the sky through the windshield. What do you see?"

Molly leaned forward on her seat and looked up. "Wha' am I lookin' for?" Molly asked.

"Satellites. The satellites tell the lady in the phone what to tell us."

"It's too deep for me, girl."

Ann laughed. "It's deep for all of us, but you must grasp everything around you and understand what everything means. You're going to be a great attorney, and you have to use your head as a file cabinet to store away bits and pieces of facts and information until your cup runneth over.

"Okay, we're ready to go. We'll call her Margaret. She's going to tell us how to get to Pinkie's uncle's house."

Ann followed instructions from her phone until they arrived at the destination.

"We're really in the country," Ann said. "That's his house way down there. It's like on a service road, and his driveway turns off it. It's sort of a private drive. How far would you think the house is from where we are?"

Molly scratched her head, then held one finger up as if to test the wind. "Two hundred feet," she said quickly, sounding positive.

Ann looked at her and smiled. "Two hundred feet, huh? I would say you're pretty close, and with the leaves beginning to fall, we're not going to be able to get close to the house without making a lotta crunching sounds."

"We may haf to watch through your binoculars," Molly said.

"Yeah, you're right. We can park in the path that the mail truck has made on its way to the mailbox, and that little clump of trees would hide us from cars going to the house and coming out," Ann said.

"We're stayin' all night?" Molly asked.

"We are," Ann said.

"What if we haf to use the restroom?" Molly asked.

"You see that clump of trees in front of us?" Ann said.

"Yeah."

"See that big tree on the right with its branches hanging down to the road?"

"Yeah."

"That's your restroom. Mine is that tree on the left with the big branch hanging out toward the road," Ann said.

Molly looked at Ann, and her eyes opened wide. "Wha' if there's a snake in there?"

"Molly, snake season's over. If there happens to be a straggler just do like we did on the mountain…take a stick and throw it outta your bathroom," Ann said in an effort to ease Molly's anxiety while knowing snake season was just beginning.

Molly jerked to look at her and then burst out laughing. After a moment, she said, "Ain't gettin' within twenty feet of a snake so throwin' it out with a stick ain't on the menu."

Ann laughed. "Okay, just yell, and I'll come and do it. Just don't loud yell too loud 'cause we don't want Pinkie to find out two broads are on a stakeout."

"Right," Molly said with a serious tone.

"Do you think you can go to sleep about eight o'clock?" Ann asked.

"I think so. Why eight?"

"I'll keep watch until midnight, and then I'll wake you, and you can keep watch until four. Wake me at four. If you want to nap until seven, you can. If you want to stay awake, that's okay too."

"If we see anything, should we take a picture with our phone?" Molly asked.

"Absolutely. Take as many as you can. Hey! Hey! What's this?" Ann said.

Molly looked up. Seeing a dark-colored pickup truck turning into the private drive to the uncle's house, she grabbed the binoculars. "Here're your glasses," she said in a hurried voice to Ann.

"Hurry and take pictures," Ann said, and then she took the binoculars and looked at the pickup. "Well, well, well," she said in a low voice.

"I got at least six pictures," Molly said.

"We left his ID description at home," Ann said, her voice sounding her frustration, "but I still saw him. He's certainly not the uncle. No! No! He's like middle age with a scar in the middle of his right cheek and a mole on his forehead. He's driving a Ford pickup with a license plate that ends with 967."

"Do you want hard copies made of the pictures?"

"Would you?" Ann said.

"Of course. How soon?" Molly asked.

"How about after lunch tomorrow? We can have a short meeting at the café."

"That'll work. I need to help Kate get ready for lunch and work through lunch if we leave here in time," Molly said.

"We'll do it," Ann said. "Will you feel like working tomorrow after hanging out here all night?"

"Oh, yeah. I used to live beside the river, you kno'," Molly said.

"I remember. I'm going to get a look at that house before it gets dark," Ann said, lifting the binoculars to her eyes again. "Well, I don't see anything interesting except for that big tree hugging the house." Her words came slow, and her voice was low. "There's a huge limb that hangs out and covers most of the house. Here. Take a look."

Molly took the binoculars, held them up, and looked. "That may be a way we can get in th' house, girl."

"To do what?" Ann said.

"When it gets dark, we could climb that tree, go out on that limb, and jump off on the roof," Molly said.

"And do what?"

"Well, you're th' chief. I'm jus' a worker. I'm not supposed to kno' wha' to do."

Ann looked at her and burst out laughing. "Do you know you're full of it?"

"Me? I don' kno' what you're talkin' about," Molly said, and then she jerked up. "Hey! Hey! A man's comin' outta the house. Look through the glasses!"

Ann took the binoculars and looked. She was quiet for a moment, and then she said, "It's Pinkie. He has a large mole in the center of his forehead. There's no doubt."

"Do we go get 'em?" Molly asked.

"We're not prepared to get him. We're only on stakeout. We'll watch through the night," Ann said.

"Do you think it's okay if I inspect the bathroom?" Molly asked.

"Just bend down and keep your head below that fence line. Check mine out if you don't mind," Ann said.

Molly crouched down, walked to the clump of trees, and returned a few moments later. "They both look good. There're no snakes, and I didn't even see a spider or a bug. There is sumpin' funny though."

"What's that?" Ann asked.

"It looks like sumpin' been sleepin' in there. There's some sage brush, an' it's all crushed down…looks like a big bowl," Molly said.

"That would be deer. They have ticks. The beds you saw are full of ticks. You sure don't want to use the restroom in there."

Molly grabbed her head with both hands. "Wha! What're we goin' to do?" Her voice was loud and anxious.

"What's on this side of the trees?" Ann asked.

"I didn't look, but the ticks'll be there too, won't they?"

"Could be. These tracks to the mailbox go right past those trees. As long as we stay on the gravel tracks, we should be okay. You take the track on the right side, and I'll take the left side," Ann said.

"Girl, I never knowed this stakeout business could be so primitive," Molly said.

"Molly, we're after bad people and wherever they go, we go."

The day waned on, and the sun slid below the horizon. Ann took the first watch and listened as Molly slept, making hissing sounds every time she inhaled. When she exhaled, her lips vibrated and air rushed out, making a whishing sound as it escaped her mouth. It was quite entertaining and provided some amusement that replaced the dullness of the night.

Except for Molly's sleep routine, the night was quiet, and there was no activity at the house.

Ann awakened Molly at midnight.

"Wha…"

"Rise and shine, girl."

Molly's head and body jerked awkwardly. "Wha…wha…?"

"Hey, hey. Everything's okay. You've been sleeping," Ann said.

Molly yawned and stretched her legs. "We're on stakeout. Right?" she said, her voice low and her words slow to develop.

"We are. Are you ready for your turn to watch the house?" Ann asked.

"Ready and wide awake."

Ann laughed.

"Anything happen?"

"Not one sound. Not one movement. Everything was so quiet that I was at the screaming point."

"Well, it's time for your nap, girl."

"You got it. Good night," Ann said, and then she scooted down in her seat and got comfortable.

The next four hours passed without incident, and Molly awakened Ann at four o'clock.

"Anything happen?" Ann asked.

"Quiet as a mouse. My turn for a nap," Molly said.

"I'll wake you later," Ann said.

"Good night," Molly said.

Ann looked through the darkness for the next hour and a half. She contemplated the hundreds of thoughts that popped up in her head. The combination of quietness and darkness created the environment for some weird thoughts.

Her phone showed the time to be five o'clock. Thinking the sun would pop up in an hour and a half created good thoughts.

Suddenly, lights came up the driveway from the house.

"Whoa," she said in a muffled voice, and then she looked at Molly who was making her sleeping noises.

Looking back toward the lights, she said, "I wish you could see this, Molly. We got Pinkie leaving his comfortable house and going somewhere to work. He doesn't know it, but we're going to be just a short distance behind him."

Ann waited for the pickup to get onto the main road, and then she followed with her lights still turned off.

The pickup turned west and traveled at a moderate rate of speed. Ann stayed behind at what she thought was a distance that the driver of the pickup wouldn't notice her.

When they had traveled for what Ann guessed to be ten miles, the pickup turned into the parking area of a building that was situated near the road.

Ann pulled onto the shoulder of the road, stopped her vehicle, took the binoculars, and surveyed the building. A sign attached to the building attracted her attention. "Security Company," it read.

"No!" she yelled.

Molly jerked up from her sleep. Her eyes bulged from her forehead and reflected bright rays of light from her pupils that came from the birth of another day as it stole its way into the car and magically white-washed the darkness. "Wha's wrong? Wha's wrong?" she asked, her words sounding fearful and anxious.

"Oh, you're awake," Ann said. "Sorry about that. While you snoozed, Pinkie left his house and went to work…went to work at a security company."

"A security company?" Molly said, her voice sounding sleepy and barely audible.

"Yeah. Remember your friend Ann used to work for a security company…the place in New York you know, and she wound up living on the bank of the Cumberland River. The security company sent several goons to come looking for her. Remember?"

"That wuz you. I remember," Molly said.

"Okay, we're outta here," Ann said, and then she drove back onto the road toward Franklin.

"Molly, do you know what we're going to do right after tomorrow's meeting?"

"No, ma'am."

"Before Pinkie gets off work, we're going to mosey down to his house and install some equipment on his property."

"You got my attention."

"You know that big tree beside his house?"

"Yeah, the one tha' has that big branch hangin' over the roof of the house."

"You're right. Well, I'm gonna climb that tree while you keep an eye out watching for any nosy person that might wander down the driveway."

"You're gonna climb th' tree?"

"Yeah, and when I get up there, I'm gonna climb out on that limb and install a pulley on it. Then I'm gonna run a rope from the pulley to the main tree."

"Whatcha gonna do that for?"

"Pinkie works for a security company. We don't know what kind of security he has around the house. But I'd be willing to bet that he doesn't have any on the roof. I just may be up there one of these days while you're off getting your education."

"Will you help me…I mean, with my studies?"

Ann looked at her, hesitated for a moment, and said, "Of course, I'll help you, and the perfect place for us to study is down by the river…you know, where we spent part of our lives, and you took a swim."

Molly laughed. "Yeah, I almost miss it."

"We got a great education, didn't we?"

"We did."

"There's something I want to do when we get down to the river."

"Wha's that?"

"I want to stop at the church."

"You're goin' to church?" Molly asked, her voice filled with disbelief.

"It's something special. You'll see. Hey! We're home."

CHAPTER 7

Ann arrived at the café at one-thirty. It was the day after the third stakeout. Most of the lunch crowd had eaten and returned to their workplace. She walked to the corner table that was isolated from the main dining room and used by the staff when business was slow.

"Hi, my daughter," Kate said, then she embraced her.

"You missed me?" Ann asked.

Kate laughed. "Yeah, you've been gone twenty hours. It's been so lonely without you. Another two hours and I would have gone looney."

Ann looked at her mother for a moment, and then she burst out laughing.

"Okay, you two," Molly said as she approached the table.

"Here's the lady that slept while I did surveillance," Ann said after recovering from her laughter.

"Whoa! Whoa! What she says is half-truth. We took turns sleeping."

"Yeah, I'm tailing Pinkie down the road, and my partner is trying to sit upright in her seat while she snores so loud the roof of my car goes up and down."

"Well, I got th' pictures, partner," Molly said, her words coming slowly and sounding playful.

"Children, children, I leave you alone for a few minutes, and you're acting like schoolchildren that have been locked up in solitary confinement," Sara said as she approached the table.

"We were just waiting for you, Mother," Kate said. "Someone asked who the best mother in the world is, and someone nominated you."

"Well, that someone is one smart cookie. Have we started the meeting?"

"Waiting for you," Kate said.

"Then the first subject would be Pinkie. What's the latest on him?"

"Grandmother, as you know, Molly and I did our third stakeout last night at Pinkie's uncle's house in Triune. About six, who comes home? Pinkie. Molly got pictures of him," Ann said.

"Here they are," Molly said, and then she gave the pictures to Sara.

Sara looked at the pictures and gave them to Kate.

"What's the next step?" Sara asked.

"Molly and I are going out there later today. The uncle's house is about two hundred feet off the main road. There's a large tree close to the house, and one of its limbs hangs directly over the house. I'm going up the tree and attach a pulley to the limb just in case I need to get on or off the roof in a hurry."

"That could be a challenge," Kate said.

"Well, we really don't know if he has cameras, but it makes sense he would, don't you think?" Ann said.

"I think that's a real sound assumption," Sara said. "What's the next step after you install the pulley?"

"We have to decide the method of apprehension," Ann said.

"I think you're right, honey. Why don't you finish your job with the pulley and observe the place tonight. After that, we should move. What do you think, Kate?" Sara asked.

"I think Ann installs the pulley, watches the place tonight, and then we get together and make a plan. We should move without delay…get this one behind us."

"Agreed," Sara said. "Ann and Molly?"

"Agreed," Ann said.

"Me too," Molly said.

"It's unanimous," Sara said. "Shall we meet here tomorrow…same time?"

"I'll be here," Kate said.

"Same here," Ann said.

"Me too," Molly said.

"When will you be ready?" Ann asked, looking at Molly.

"Have to finish th' dishes. Will three be okay?"

"Three it is. Good. That'll give me time to run to the shop and get a pulley and some rope," Ann said.

Everyone went their separate ways.

Ann went to her produce company headquarters, got a pulley, and then returned to the café.

Molly met her at the door. "Ready to go," she said.

"I'm going to the restroom," Ann said. "Will you please ask mother to give us two sandwiches and four bottles of water?"

"Will do," Molly said.

They separated then met again a few minutes later.

Kate met them. "Please be careful," she said. "I can't afford to lose my best helper, and I can't afford to lose my only daughter. Got it?"

"Got it," Ann and Molly said in unison, and then they left the café.

"Molly, would you mind keeping an eye on Pinkie while I install the pulley?" Ann asked.

"Happy to. How do we do it?" Molly asked.

"We need another vehicle. We can go to the produce company and get a pickup truck or go down First Avenue and borrow the city car."

"I'd rather use the city car," Molly said.

"We're on our way," Ann said, and then she drove to First Avenue and parked behind the city car that she had used so many times during the time she lived as a homeless person on the banks of the Cumberland River. The city car was a complementary vehicle provided by the city for use by any authorized individual.

"Okay, let me borrow your phone," Ann said.

Molly looked at her with a puzzled look but gave her phone to Ann.

"I'm putting Pinkie's work address in the GPS. Once you get there, you'll see the security company's name on the sign facing the street. Find an inconspicuous place to watch and text me if you see Pinkie leave," Ann said, and then she gave the phone to Molly.

"Got it. Anything else?"

"Text me when you're in place."

"Will do. Don't leave until I get th' city car started," Molly said.

"I'll wait until you get on the road. Your phone is probably gonna tell you to drive down I-65. I'm going through Nolensville, but I'll wait until I hear from you."

"Talk to ya later," Molly said, and then she went to the city car, got in, and drove away.

"Showtime," Ann said, and then she drove by her house, got a nine-millimeter, and continued to Triune.

Thirty minutes passed, and then Ann pulled into the space where she and Molly had parked the night before. Five minutes later, she got a text that Molly was in place.

"Car, let's go down and see Pinkie," Ann said, and then she drove to the house where Pinkie had stayed the night before. She pulled her blouse from her jeans to allow some slack, and then she unbuttoned the bottom button, slid the nine-millimeter through the open blouse so that it rested on the top part of her jeans, and then rebuttoned the blouse.

Getting up the tree will be no problem, she thought, but two limbs crossed and blocked access to the one that hung over the house. *I could climb above them and lower myself headfirst onto the big limb, but the nine-mil would drop out and shoot me,* she thought.

Okay, I'm a woman, and it's time to start thinking like one, she thought, and then she slid back down the tree to the ground. Starting to walk to her car, she looked back at the two limbs. Opening the trunk lid, she pulled out the rope she had gotten at the produce company.

"Sure would be great if I had something to put on the ground. Oh well, maybe it's soft," she said, and then she slid under the car and tied one end of the rope to the frame of the car. Once the rope was secure, she scooted out, took the other end, climbed the tree, and tied it to the smallest limb.

Climbing down, she walked to her car, started it, pulled the gearshift to drive, and then she depressed the gas pedal very gently. Looking back, she decided the limb wasn't breaking. "It's just like driving in the snow," she said. "You have to be patient and keep on driving." Suddenly, the car lunged forward. "Whoa! I think I did it," she said, and then she got out of the car to look. All the time she was thinking the limb may have gone through the roof of the house. Much to her amazement, it was still attached to the tree but hanging down away from its sister branch.

She cut off the engine and untied the rope. "I'm running behind," she said and then hurried to the car trunk, got the pulley, a three-foot piece of rope, and rushed to the tree. Looking at the pulley, she questioned how she was going to climb the tree and hold on to the pulley. Thinking for a moment, she spoke with a positive tone. "I can be a carpenter." With that declaration, she slid one end of the rope through a belt loop, looped it through the axle of the pulley, and tied the ends of the rope together.

"Up I go," she said, and then she grabbed a bottom limb and pulled herself up until she climbed to the roof of the house. Looking at the limb that grew over the house, she was surprised how close it was to the roof. "That won't work at all," she said. Searching for a solution, she looked up. "Whoa! Where did you come from?" She looked toward a limb about four feet above the limb near the roof. Her eyes enlarged, and a smile flashed onto her face. A large limb grew at an angle away from the main limb creating a V-looking part of the tree. It was a perfect place that Mother Nature had made for the pulley to be mounted.

Loosening the knot in the rope that ran through her belt loop, she rerouted it through the V-part of the tree limb, then through the axle of the pulley, and tied the ends together.

"I have to get outta here," she said outloud to herself. "Pinkie's gonna come home any minute."

She hurriedly climbed down the tree, ran to her car, and then drove up the driveway at a high rate of speed. When she had driven the length of the driveway, she drove to the space where she had parked the last night. She was surprised to see the city car parked there. *What is Molly doing here?* she thought. *She didn't text me. What's going on?*

Slowly and carefully, she opened her car door and walked to the city car. Peering inside, she was puzzled that Molly was not in the car. *Maybe she went to the restroom,* but there was no visible sign of her. Suddenly, she noticed a sheet of paper on the passenger's seat. Looking in all directions to satisfy herself that she was alone, she opened the door and got the note. It had been written with a heavy ink marking pen and was scribbled—whether to disguise the handwriting or simply because the writer didn't have a good technique, Ann couldn't guess.

Ann tilted the note so she would have better light. It took time to decipher the words, but finally she read: "Have your watchdog. Leave two hundred fifty thousand dollars one hundred feet from house at six p.m. day after tomorrow. If you don't, you will lose your watchdog."

Squeezing the note, Ann looked in all directions, and then walked to her car, got in, and drove to Kate's house.

Getting out of her car, she now felt she was the one being watched. She wasn't scared, just irritated…irritated that she would allow herself to be so careless as to be cornered like a helpless mouse.

"Sweetheart…"

"Mother, Molly. He took Molly! Pinkie took Molly!"

"But…but how? How did you get separated for Molly to be taken?"

"Molly was watching the place where Pinkie works while I was installing a pulley on the tree limb above Pinkie's house. When I finished, I found her car at the end of the driveway…empty…with the note on the car seat."

"I better call Mother," Kate said, and then she picked up her phone and called Sara. After talking only for a few moments, she put the phone down and said, "Mother's on the way."

"I just hate to face her knowing I let someone take Molly."

"Honey, we're dealing with thugs. They're not going to throw up their hands and welcome us into their world."

A few moments passed, and Sara joined them. Ann repeated the story she had told Kate.

"It's time to vote the marbles again," Sara said, her face showing no emotion. "Kate, are the cup and marbles in the kitchen?"

"Yes, on the right side of the coffeemaker."

"Good. I'll vote first," Sara said, and then she went to the kitchen. A few moments passed, and she returned. "I voted. Who's next?"

"You go, Mother. I'll go last," Ann said.

Her jaws drawn tight, causing her to appear to be serious and determined, Kate looked at Ann for a moment and then went to the kitchen. She returned quickly. "You're next," she said.

Ann moved hurriedly, voted, and then returned to meet with Sara and Kate.

"I will tally the vote," Sara said, and then she went to the kitchen, stepping at a brisk pace and with authority. After a brief period, she returned. "As you remember, the first vote was two black marbles and one white marble. That vote would have given Pinkie a chance to escape the final curtain at the discretion of the person that apprehended him. This vote, the second vote, has him with three black marbles which precludes any concession to Pinkie. In other words, he is to perish when apprehended. Does anyone have any questions?" she asked, standing with her hands resting on her hips, her eyes focused on Kate and then Ann. After a few moments, she said, "What Pinkie didn't tell you is when he will return Molly. He didn't tell you he would exchange Molly for the money. What Pinkie plans to do is get the money and then destroy Molly. What we're dealing with is a scumbag that has less compassion than a snake. We must get the money to him and keep him out of his house until we know Molly's fate."

"Grandmother, we only have forty-eight hours. Meanwhile, how much abuse will Pinkie inflict on Molly?" Ann said.

Sara looked at Ann as if she were trying to develop a solution, and then she walked to a window and looked out. It was dark, so there was nothing to see.

Ann and Kate remained silent as Sara gazed out the window. After a few moments, the silence became uncomfortable, but Ann and Kate kept their place.

Suddenly, Sara turned to look at Ann. "How good are you with that long rifle of yours?"

The question was a complete surprise, and Ann appeared confused for a moment. Finally, she said, "Are you asking if I can shoot straight…like hit something when I shoot?"

"Exactly. If I designated a target, are you proficient enough that you could hit it?"

"Grandmother, if you place an ant on the shoulder of your blouse, I can shoot it off without any damage to your blouse," Ann said.

"What about my neck?" Sara asked.

Ann looked at her, studied her eyes with her own eyes, and laughed. Gaining her composure, she said, "No damage to anything."

"Well, you're the gal I've been looking for," Sara said.

"What do you have in mind, Grandmother?"

"You were installing a pulley on Pinkie's property. Did you finish the job?"

"I did. It's located on a tree limb that grows over the roof of his house. It's functional as we speak."

"Great! Let's all go sit down at the table," Sara said, and then she took the lead and went to the kitchen.

Ann and Kate followed.

"Please have a seat, ladies," Sara said.

Ann and Kate seated themselves.

"Okay, we'll take care of Pinkie day after tomorrow night. That'll be Friday night. Ann, will you arrange for a block of ice, eight inches thick, two feet wide, and two feet long to be delivered to Pinkie's house Friday at five-thirty? Also, we need it to stay intact, so we need it to be packed in dry ice. Then we'll need to unload it, so can you transport it in your box truck…the one with the hydraulic loading arm. Add a two-foot by two-foot piece of plywood that's three quarters of an inch thick," Sara said.

"Block of ice, eight inches thick, two feet wide, two feet long, load it in the box truck with the hydraulic arm. Throw in a two-by-two square of plywood that's three quarters of an inch thick. Got it," Ann said.

"That's step one. Step two is a question. Do you think you can get on Pinkie's roof before five thirty Friday with your rifle?"

"Not a problem. Looking at his house straight on, there's a giant tree on the right side that prevents anyone being seen. I'll be on the roof before five thirty. What do I do once I'm on the roof?"

"About to let you know. Kate and I will leave two hundred and fifty thousand dollars on the driveway one hundred feet from Pinkie's front door. I'll leave the briefcase open so the money will stick out like a sore thumb. We'll withdraw and stay out of sight. Pinkie will slither out of his house, down the driveway, and then he'll get the briefcase. When he starts back, I want you to shoot him in the right thigh…get just enough to cause him to stop in his tracks. Kate and I will rush in, retrieve the money, and corral Pinkie."

"What if he has a weapon or what if he hobbles to the house with the money?" Ann asked.

"If he shows a weapon, shoot it out of his hand. If he starts hobbling or running, shoot the other thigh," Sara said. "Now, what about the uncle?"

"I think Pinkie lives alone. There are absolutely no signs of an uncle. As soon as I see that you have Pinkie, I'm off the roof and into the house to get Molly," Ann said.

"Let's hope Pinkie's keeping Molly inside the house, and he hasn't harmed her," Kate said.

"What if he's hiding her some other place?" Sara said.

"If Molly's not in the house, Pinkie will have more than a shot in the thigh," Ann said.

"How're we arranging transportation?" Kate asked.

"Do you mind driving?" Sara asked.

"Of course, I'll drive."

"I'll drive the box truck and park just outside the driveway," Ann said. "You can park behind me, Mother. What is the plan about the ice?"

"I'll take care of that," Sara said. "Just park and get on the roof. And remember, shoot him in the right thigh. Do not, I repeat, do not shoot to kill him."

"I'll just shoot an inch off his thigh, Grandmother," Ann said.

"Good. You have things to do tomorrow, and your mother and I have some financial matters to get ready, so I'm going to bid both of you goodnight," Sara said.

"Mother, I'll watch until you get home," Kate said.

"Goodnight, Mother. Goodnight, Grandmother," Ann said, and then she went home and turned in for the night.

CHAPTER 8

Ann awakened at four-thirty. She looked at the clock and took a deep breath. Not only was it too early to get up, but she felt bad from lack of sleep. Having tossed and tumbled most of the night, she felt she had just completed two marathons back-to-back.

The thought of getting to Pinkie's house without being seen was troubling. She had acted nonchalant when she talked with her grandmother. In fact, she had acted so casually that as she thought about the conversation, she really berated herself.

"Okay, let's ask the computer," she said, and then she went to the computer and searched for briar-proof clothing. Sure enough, she found exactly what she thought she needed. Surprised at her find, she felt considerable relief.

It's ten after five. What do I do now? she wondered as lingering bouts of exhaustion from lack of sleep clouded her thoughts. *Take a shower, have breakfast, and go to the shop,* she decided.

Having settled on an agenda, she proceeded with her plan. She left home at six-thirty, stopped and got two large coffees and a dozen donuts, then drove to the produce company office where she met Dave, the general manager.

"I brought you coffee and donuts," Ann said.

"Uh, oh," Dave said. "When the boss brings you coffee and donuts, there's somethin' brewing."

Ann smiled. "Well, I have to confess. I do need some things." Dressed in form-fitting, dark slacks and a white silk blouse, she appeared glamorous and stunning. Her auburn hair, appearing more reddish in the morning light, flowed around her shoulders, creating an even more striking appearance.

"I'm going on a selling mission, and I need a box truck that has a hydraulic lift. I also need a block of ice…yes, a certain size, of course. It has to be eight inches thick and two feet wide by two feet long…a square, if you will. Oh yes, I need dry ice in a rubberized container to keep it chilly and intact. Do you think you can get all that for me?"

"Of course. When do you want these items?"

"Tomorrow at two o'clock. Oh! I need a two-by-two-foot piece of plywood that's three quarters of an inch thick."

"Sounds like you're going on a speaking tour and want to stay cool."

Ann laughed. "Does sound that way, doesn't it? Well, you can't sell lettuce unless it's green and chilly, can you?"

Dave touched his forehead with the palm of his hand. "Of course not. We're not the greatest produce company because we sell brown lettuce."

Ann laughed again. "No, sir, we're great because we do what is common sense. We ask ourselves, 'what would I buy?' and then we do everything to fill the bill. That's a menu for success."

"That's great! Do you want to give everyone a pep talk? They'd love it…coming from you."

"And I would love to do it. The problem is that I have a dozen irons in the fire for a coupla days. After that, it'll be coffee and donuts for everyone," Ann said.

"Sounds great. I'll have all your items ready at two o'clock tomorrow," Dave said.

"Great! I'll see you then," Ann said, waving a hand as she turned to leave.

Back in the car, she buckled in and drove to the outdoors store at the mall. Going into the store, she looked around for an employee. Seeing a man wearing a store badge, she said, "Sir, can you help me?"

"Give me a minute, miss, and I'll be right back."

Ann backed up against a display table and waited. Only a few seconds passed before the man returned.

"Hi, my name's Chuck. How may I help you?" he said as his eyes inspected every inch of Ann's face, and then his eyes dropped to look at the upper part of her body.

Ann smiled to herself as she observed Chuck's very noticeable admiration. "Chuck, I'm going hiking with some friends, and they say we'll be going through some terrible underbrush. It's populated with those big, awful thorns. As you can see when you look closely at me, I'm not a hunter. Nor do I make a habit of wading through weeds, brushes, and thorns. Actually, I'm just a city girl. You with me?"

"Yes, ma'am!" Chuck said, his voice high-pitched and sounding as if he had been stuck with a needle. "I mean, yes…yes, I do understand," he said a little more calmly.

"Good. So, what would you suggest that would keep me from those nasty, sharp thorns that are laden with bacteria?"

"I think…I mean I think I know just the thing. Follow me, please," Chuck said. He started off, then stopped abruptly and turned to look at Ann. "Oh, I'm sorry. I didn't mean follow me, like…" he said, and then he struggled for words.

"No problem, Chuck. I'm following you because you know where everything is located."

He looked at her for a moment, and then he smiled and said, "I'm sorry. You're, well, you're the most beautiful woman I've ever seen, and it's hard to keep my feet on the ground."

"Well, I'm more than flattered, Chuck, but we'll get through this. We were on our way to look at clothing that'll guarantee a safe walk through a briar patch."

"Yes...yes, briar patch...I mean clothing. There they are on the rack straight ahead," Chuck said, pointing to a rack stocked with brown-colored clothing.

Ann went to the display and looked at the clothing. Turning to look at Chuck, she said, "I think you're right. This stuff is like canvas. A rocket couldn't penetrate it."

Chuck smiled awkwardly. "So, it's what you were thinking you wanted?"

Ann hesitated for a moment as if she were processing what Chuck said. "I think it's what I was thinking I needed," she said. "I'll try these for a fit." She took an armful of pants and shirts to the dressing room.

After selecting a pair of pants and a shirt, she returned to meet Chuck. "I'll take these. Now, I need a pair of boots that'll break a snake's tooth if it chooses to try to make a meal of my leg."

Chuck's eyes moved to look at Ann's legs. "Uh, boots...right," he said. "Uh, do you...I mean what size do you wear?"

"Size seven."

"Okay, let's go up in size a little bit...just a little bit because they're boots, you know. I'll be right back," Chuck said before rushing away.

A few moments later, he returned with two boxes. Pulling out a boot from one of the boxes, he said, "These open on the sides. That way, you don't have to struggle...I mean they're easy to open. You buckle 'em up this way." He attempted to secure one of the buckles, but his hands were so unsteady that the buckle refused to lock.

"Let me try," Ann said, easily closing one of the buckles.

Chuck watched, but his face was flush, and his eyes were still and lifeless.

Ann put on one boot, then the second one, and then she walked back and forth. "These will do just fine," she said. "Do you have snake guards that will fit me?"

"Uh, yes, yes, we have just the thing. I'll be right back," Chuck said. He left but returned quickly with a package. "You wanna try these? They strap on to the front of your...your legs."

"Let me try them," Ann said. She buckled the guards over the front of her pants legs. "Great! Now, a pair of long-sleeve leather gloves."

"We have them," Chuck said. He rushed away and once again returned quickly.

"Ah! I'm finished," Ann said. She paid for the merchandise, left the store, and drove home where she spent the remainder of the day cleaning her AR-15 rifle and nine-millimeter handgun. When she finished, she gently placed them on the couch.

Kate called at four-thirty.

"Hi, Mother."

"Honey, we need to talk about tomorrow night. Your grandmother will be here in fifteen minutes. Can you come over?"

"I'll be there in fifteen minutes," Ann said, and then she got ready and went to Kate's house.

"Come in, honey. Grandmother's already here."

Ann followed her mother to the living room where Sara was seated and having tea.

"Hi, honey. You look so nice tonight," Sara said.

"Thank you, Grandmother. You look rested. How do you feel?" Ann asked.

"I never felt better. I got a wonderful night's sleep last night. Are you ready to talk about tomorrow night?" Sara asked.

"I am. Do you want to lead the way?" Ann said.

"You go first. What have you done to get prepared?"

"I'm to pick up the box truck with ice, dry ice, plywood, one fifteen-foot strip of rope, and one thirty-foot, tomorrow at two. I also went shopping…bought briar-proof pants and shirt, boots, snake-guard shields, and elbow-length leather gloves. When you and Mother show up at Pinkie's, I'll be sitting on his roof with my rifle and a nine-millimeter."

"Honey, you thought of everything. I'm so proud to have you as a daughter," Kate said.

"Oh, shush," Ann said.

Kate and Sara laughed.

"Your mother and I plan to be in the driveway one hundred feet from Pinkie's house at five-fifteen. We have a metal box with the money in it, but we'll take some of the bills and let them hang out over the top of the box. It's just a way to make a money-hungry fool drool. Whatever you do, honey, don't shoot Pinkie to put him away. Shoot him in the upper thigh just on the outside of his thigh to make him limp," Sara said. "I know I'm repeating myself, but repetition is a memory-clincher."

"What if he runs, Grandmother?"

"Shoot 'em in the other thigh. As soon as he's disabled, we have to get in that house. If Molly's not there, we'll have to work on Pinkie," Sara said.

"For Pinkie's sake, Molly better be in the house tied to a chair or something and unharmed."

"We understand," Kate said.

"Well, I think everyone has their marching orders. Does anyone have a question?" Sara asked.

Kate and Ann told Sara they had no questions, and they would all meet at Pinkie's house the next night. Ann accompanied Sara home, and then she went to her own home.

The night passed, and Ann was up early. She thought about her schedule for the day, but it seemed difficult to organize everything, so she decided to go jogging. Getting dressed in her running gear only took a few moments, so she was out the door and running before she changed her mind.

As she ran, it was as if she had a mirror in front of her. The problem was that she wasn't seeing herself, she was seeing Molly. It alarmed her.

Remembering the two men who raped Cynthia, the trauma she endured, and the subsequent coma, caused her to believe the worst for Molly. There was no indication that Pinkie would return Molly in the same condition that she was before she was grabbed.

He's abused her for sure, Ann thought. *Molly's being tortured and abused, and Pinkie's just walking around as if he has all the cards and is invincible.*

Coming to an abrupt stop, she turned and ran back home where she immediately unfolded the clothing she was to wear later in the day. Having tried it on already, she still undressed and tried it on again.

Walking from the bedroom to the living room then back again, she could see in her mind the briars and bushes on the right side of the driveway that led to Pinkie's uncle's house.

Pulling at her pants while holding them in a tight grasp, she was satisfied they were sufficient to protect her from the briars.

Her phone rang. She looked at it and declined the call. The time showed ten-thirty. She went to the refrigerator, got a bottle of orange juice, and sipped on it. Deciding to clear her head, she sat in a side chair and stretched both legs straight out. Closing her eyes, she tried to relax, but she slouched down in the chair and then straightened up over and over.

To pass the time, she called Sara. "Hey, Grandmother, it's your favorite granddaughter. Just called to see if we're on schedule."

"I think I know you, and I know why you called."

"You do?"

"I do," Sara said.

"Can you fill me in?" Ann asked.

"I can, and I will. You called because you're getting antsy, and you wanted to kill some time."

Ann laughed. "How'd you get so wise?" Her words came slowly to emphasize the question but also to highlight her belief that Sara was so wise.

"I walked in your shoes forty years ago. I know your every thought, your every temptation, and your every desire. I'm just an older Ann."

Ann held out the telephone in front of her and gazed at it. After a moment, she heard her grandmother's voice asking if Ann was still on the phone with her.

"Sorry, Grandmother, you stunned me," Ann said.

"I didn't mean to frighten you. I just wanted to remind you that we're made from the same cloth. You are precious to me, and you share my heart."

"Whew," Ann said, breathing loudly. "I'm glad I share your heart. I'll take good care of my part."

"Good. Do you want to come over and have a sandwich with me? Your mother has someone covering for her at the cafe, and she'll be here too."

"I'd be delighted," Ann said. "I have to change clothes, and I'll be right over. See you then."

Ann changed clothes and went to her grandmother's house. Kate arrived a few minutes later. They had lunch, talked about Pinkie, and then talked small talk for an hour.

"Oh, my! Oh, my!" Ann said loudly. "It's nearly two o'clock! I have to get the truck." She kissed her mother and grandmother on the cheek and rushed to the door. "See you tonight," she said quickly as she sped out of the house.

Driving fast, she arrived at the produce company, got the box truck, and drove home. It was two-forty-five. She reminded herself she only had fifteen minutes to change clothes.

Hurrying, she rushed into her house, changed into the briar-proof pants and shirt, and pulled on the boots. After that, she buckled the snake guards around her legs, put on a baseball cap, made a ponytail of her hair, and pulled it through the space behind the cap.

Hurrying once again, she strapped on her nine-millimeter, picked up the carrying case for her AR-15 rifle and suppressors for both weapons, and then she placed the rifle and suppressors in the case.

Grabbing the night goggles and leather gloves, she hurriedly placed them in a second carrying case.

Picking up both cases, she looked around the room and mentally took inventory of everything she had and was supposed to have.

Satisfied, she left her house, put the bags in the truck, and drove to Triune. It was ten minutes before four.

I only have an hour and a half, she thought as she pulled the truck into the spot just off the main road. She didn't want Pinkie to notice the truck. Observing the house, she didn't see any movement, so she got out of the truck, took out the two bags, and started walking into the brush and briars that bordered the right side of the driveway that ended at Pinkie's uncle's house. She thought that was the necessary route to avoid being seen.

Progress was slow. Even with her briar-proof clothing, briars lunged at her face, and the brush created a barrier to prevent her from pulling her bags through. She felt so handicapped because she had to hold the bags, she had no use of her hands and couldn't decide how to get herself and baggage through the extreme brush. She thought about taking one bag close to the house and leaving one behind to take on a separate trip. That would mean fighting the brush two times, so she vetoed that proposal.

Looking toward the house, she took a deep breath and plowed forward. A branch from a tall briar pricked her cheek on the left side of her face just below her earlobe. "No! No!" she shrieked. Instant pain shot through her face. Wanting not to know her worst fears, she touched her cheek with two fingers anyway. Feeling her wet cheek, she jerked her hand down and looked at it. Blood covered her fingers and drained down into her palm. "No! No! Oh, no!" she shrieked again, her voice now sounding anxious. Suddenly remembering she had a first aid kit, she wriggled around two stands of brush and finally opened the bag that held the first aid kit. Blood was now dripping off her cheek.

Grabbing a package of gauze, she stripped off the protective paper using her teeth. Dabbing her face, she quickly opened a large fabric bandage, peeled off the wrapper, and stuck it over what she believed to be the cut on her face. The dripping stopped so she thought she must've been lucky and stuck the bandage in the right place.

"Okay, Pinkie, now I'm really mad," she said tersely as she grabbed her bags and waded into the brush. "A hundred feet, and I'll be there," she said in a low voice.

Long, slender saplings slapped her face as she forged ahead. Short, tough bushes snagged her feet as she fought for every foot in front of her. It was four-thirty. She believed it would take another fifteen minutes to get alongside the house and then several additional minutes to get into position. That would make her very close to the appointed time of five-thirty.

Because of her determination, fighting the stubborn brush simply became an irritant, and soon she broke out into the opening that surrounded the house. The tree that grew close to the house was only a few feet ahead. Hurrying to it, she looked up to the roof. *How am I going up and bringing the bags at the same time?* she thought. *Okay, I'll go up first, get the rope, come down, tie the bags to it, pull the bags up, and then I'll go back up.*

The process worked just as planned, and soon she and the bags were on the roof. Carefully removing the rifle and the night goggles, she placed the rifle strap over her shoulder, picked up the goggles, and crawled carefully to the eve of the house. Below her, the driveway stretched out toward the street.

Suddenly, she had a thought. *I can't use the rifle. I'd blow his entire leg off. I need to use the nine mil.* Scooting back to the bag, she lowered the rifle, pulled out the nine-millimeter, and crawled back to the eve.

Once again, she looked down at the driveway then jerked back. *It's Grandmother!* The thought exploded in her head. *She's too early! She's too early! This will just foul up the works! No! No!* The words screamed in her thoughts but were all for naught, because she didn't dare make any noise. The whereabouts of Pinkie were unknown.

She looked down at the driveway. Through the shadows, she could see a dark-colored box with what appeared to be paper money scattered on top and around the box. *Well, Grandmother does everything with a little flair,* Ann thought. *If I was Pinkie, I sure would be tempt-*

ed just to run out and grab that box and all the greenbacks scattered around it.

The ridge of the roof caused discomfort to her chest area, so she used her knees and forearms to lift herself slightly. Then she rolled to her right side to shift more weight to that side.

Suddenly, a sharp-burning pain erupted below her left armpit. Wincing, she grabbed the area with her right hand and twisted the top part of her body repeatedly to ease the pain. She held her bottom lip tightly between her teeth.

Twisting her body must have helped because the burning sensation began to be less severe. As she continued to twist, a faint noise sounded below her. Ignoring her pain, she moved to the edge of the roof and looked down at the driveway. A figure walked toward the box Sara had left. *It's Pinkie!* Thinking that Pinkie may have sent Molly out to get the box, her thoughts froze for a moment. *No! No! He wouldn't do that. He wouldn't take a chance that Molly might run away.*

She waited. Unlike other people whose hearts would now be pounding against their chests, Ann remained calm. She lacked the genes that would trigger anxiety or emotions that dealt with death. Her heart was beating hard when she faced Big Al, but he was chasing her. The irony of her mental makeup was that there were no visible actions that would cause her to appear callous or lack empathy. She simply appeared as an intelligent, beautiful woman who had ingrained propensity for business.

Pinkie got to the box, stopped, looked toward the left then to the right, and then bent down, picked up the dark-colored box, and started walking back to the house. He wore a sweatshirt with a hood that was pulled over his head. Although dark shadows surrounded him, Ann believed without a doubt that it was a man. She lifted the nine-millimeter, focused on his right thigh, and squeezed the trigger. The figure immediately jerked backwards, stumbled, and fell viciously on his back. Only a few seconds passed before Sara and Kate appeared from the shadows, each holding a nine-millimeter pointed at the fallen person's head.

Seeing Sara and Kate had things under control, Ann moved hurriedly to the side of the house then jumped to the ground.

"Oh!" she said loudly, grabbing her left ankle. Burning pain raced up her leg, and her first thought was that she had broken her ankle. Sitting awkwardly, she held her ankle and rubbed it softly. A few moments later, the burning pain subsided somewhat, and she struggled to stand. Finally, she stood erect and hobbled around to the front of the house, climbed the steps, and went inside, holding the nine-millimeter at the ready.

The interior of the house was so dark she couldn't see. *There has to be lights,* she thought, so she felt around the wall nearest the entrance door until she found the light switch and flipped it on.

"Now, where's Molly?" she said, and then she searched every room. "She's not here! She's not here!" she yelled as she returned to the front room while sounding exasperated. Stepping quickly to leave the room, pain again surged through her foot and leg. Grabbing the door frame with her free hand, she gritted her teeth and focused all her thoughts on her ankle. "Get over it," she told herself. "We hafta find Molly."

Stepping out on the porch, she carefully shifted her weight to favor the hurt ankle, and then with a limp, she moved to stand in front of Pinkie who was still standing in the driveway visibly trembling and obviously in pain as Kate tied a tourniquet around his leg. Holding the nine-millimeter straight down by her side, she said in a calm voice, "Where's Molly?"

Pinkie looked at her for a few moments, puckered his lips, and spit in her face.

Ann didn't flinch, nor did she move.

"Here you are, sweetheart," Sara said, holding out a handkerchief.

Ann took it with her left hand and slowly wiped her eyes and face, and then she dropped it to the ground.

"Mother, move over and stand with Grandmother," Ann said, her voice still calm.

Kate stood for a moment, looked at Ann, but finally joined Sara on Pinkie's left side.

Ann lifted the nine-millimeter slowly but steadily so that the barrel was pointed straight at Pinkie, but then she moved it slightly to his right side and squeezed the trigger.

The round entered Pinkie's right bicep and exited on the opposite side. Blood shot out for a moment and then started flowing.

Pinkie trembled at a greater rate. Perspiration erupted from the pores on his face and rolled down onto his neck.

"Where's Molly?" Ann asked.

Pinkie's body continued to shake visibly, but he didn't answer.

Ann lifted her weapon and placed the barrel to Pinkie's mouth.

He jerked away from the barrel and mumbled something that was vague and jumbled.

Ann shoved the weapon closer to his mouth.

"Basement. She's in the basement," he uttered, his words broken and muffled by Ann's weapon.

She turned but the pain caused her to stop abruptly. "Oh," she groaned and then bent down to hold her ankle. *Molly's in the basement,* she thought. *She may be in distress.*

Standing upright, she said, "Let's go." Moving briskly, she ran up the steps and into the house that was still lighted from Ann's prior visit. *In the basement. Where's the basement?* she thought.

Looking quickly around the room, she noticed an empty space in one corner. Walking to it, she could see a stairwell leading to a lower floor. *A light. Now I need some light,* she thought. Noticing a light switch on the staircase wall, she walked to it and flipped the switch. The stairwell lit up. Moving carefully, she stepped to the bottom of it. Again, the area remained dark.

Feeling along the adjoining wall of the stairwell, she found the light switch and flipped it on. At first, the light blinded her, and she stood still for a moment. As her eyes adjusted, she looked about the room. It was empty except for something in a far corner. Running to it, she could see a person lying on the floor. Judging by the hair, she believed it to be Molly.

"Molly?" Ann said, and then she repeated the name with a whispering voice.

The person lay in a fetal position with her arms tied behind her with a dirty piece of bed sheet. Another piece of dirty white cloth was tied around her face, gagging her mouth.

"Molly?" Ann said again, her voice low and soft. "I know it's you. I've come to set you free." She hurriedly untied the cloth that suppressed Molly's mouth and then she untied her hands. Molly did not respond.

Ann rushed upstairs, found a paper cup, filled it with water, and rushed back to Molly. Squatting, she held the cup so that the water touched Molly's lips, and then she dabbed it across her brow and cheeks. She set the cup carefully on the floor and took Molly's shoulders and gently massaged them. Next, she held both of Molly's arms at the biceps, applied a slight bit of pressure and slid her hands down Molly's arms to her fingertips while applying the same bit of pressure. She repeated the same procedure and then again dabbed Molly's face with water.

Molly jerked.

Ann held Molly's shoulders. "Hey, it's your best friend who come to rescue you," she said in a low voice, her words coming as if in slow motion.

"Uh," Molly grunted and jerked again.

"You're okay now, Molly. Everything's okay," Ann said.

Molly grunted again, and then her eyes opened, her eyelids batting repeatedly.

"Want a drink of water?" Ann asked, her voice still low and soft.

Molly did not respond.

Ann held the paper cup to Molly's mouth and carefully tipped it so the water touched her lips. Finally, there was movement. Molly's lips moved slowly, rubbing against each other, and then opening slightly to touch the water.

"That's a girl, Molly. Just take your time," Ann said. "I'm going to hold the cup so the water touches your lips."

Molly slowly sipped the water and then whispered, "My eyes are hurtin'."

"Oh, my, my, my. We'll take care of that. Are you hungry?"

A long silence followed, and then Molly said in a quiet voice, "Yes." Her answer made three syllables out of the three-letter word.

"Do you think you can walk if I hold onto you?" Ann asked.

Another silence followed and then Molly said, "I'll try."

"Great! Let's get you standing upright." Ann put her arms underneath Molly's armpits and eased her to her feet. "Molly, we have to climb some stairs. Do you think you're up to it?"

Molly was unsteady and clung to Ann. Her eyes continued to open and close rapidly.

"Molly, let's get another drink of water. Hold onto me while I get the cup," Ann said, bending down to retrieve the cup. "After we get some water, we're gonna get you some food."

"Uh, uh," Molly groaned.

Ann held the cup while Molly took sips of water.

"Let's go," Molly said, her voice so low and weak that her words were barely audible.

"Atta girl. You have some friends upstairs, and they'll be happy to see you!" Ann said, and then she helped Molly up the stairs and out of the house into the cool air.

The change of dark to light to dark again caused a great deal of confusion to Molly, and she shook her head as if to cope with it. Her eyes opened and shut even more rapidly.

"Molly!" Kate yelled. "Mother, it's Molly!" she said as she finished tying a tourniquet around Pinkie's arm.

"Keep your nine-millimeter on Pinkie," Sara said to Kate, and then she rushed to Molly and Ann. Extending her hands slowly with a gentle motion, she took Molly's hand, held it for a moment, and said in a low voice, "How are you, Molly?"

Molly was moving in slow motion as she turned to look at Sara. Her eyes captured some moonlight, causing the pupils of her eyes to appear glazed. "I'm okay," she muttered in a slow, labored voice.

Kate joined her mother. "Shall I bring the truck down?" she said, still holding her nine-millimeter on Pinkie.

Sara looked at her through the dark shadows and said, "Yes, please. It's time. I'll watch Pinkie."

"I'll be back shortly," Kate said.

"Please be careful," Sara said.

"Mother, do you want me to go with you?" Ann said. She hobbled noticeably while attempting to shift weight from her injured ankle.

"Honey, you're hurting. I'll be okay. After we finish our business here, we'll take you to the emergency room," Kate said, and then she walked hurriedly away.

Ann turned to look at her grandmother and Molly. "Grandmother, I'm going into the house and look for some food and water. Molly needs some water and protein."

"You shouldn't be walking on that foot, honey."

"I'll be okay," Ann said, and then she walked past Pinkie and into the house. "Let's see what's in the pantry," she said. Opening the door, she was pleasantly surprised to find a six pack of canned tuna and bottled water. Checking the good-to date on the tuna, she saw that it was safe to eat, so she opened one of the cans, found a spoon, took a bottle of water, and went back to Molly. "I got a drink and some protein," she said.

Molly didn't respond.

Ann touched the water to Molly's lips and moistened her entire mouth. She then mashed the tuna into a pasty substance, dipped some out, and placed it on Molly's lips. Molly was motionless for a few moments but slowly her lips opened slightly and touched the food. Slowly and deliberately, she began taking small bites of the food. Ann gave her drops of water as she began to eat.

"Kate is here with the truck," Sara said in a voice loud enough that Ann heard her. "Can you leave Molly for a minute and throw the rope down from the roof?"

"I'm on my way," Ann said. She hobbled to the tree beside the house, climbed it to get herself onto the roof, picked up a rope that she had made a hangman's noose on the end, and threw it to the ground below.

The truck began backing up then stopped. Kate jumped down from the driver's side, opened the overhead door, and turned on the hydraulic lifting arm. "I'm going to put the package right below the eve of the house. Is that okay, Mother?" she asked.

"It's perfect," Sara said.

Operating the hydraulic lifting arm, Kate guided it to pick up a small pallet which held a two-foot square piece of plywood that in turn held a two-foot by two-foot block of ice that was eight inches thick and was covered by a towel. Another towel covered the bottom, and it sat on a second piece of two-foot piece of plywood. She then guided the arm to lower the package so that it was in front of the house and below the eve. The towels and the darkness of the night concealed the block of ice that was the major ingredient of the package.

"That is perfect, Kate. Now, it's time to get Pinkie to the hospital," Sara said. "Pinkie, you're too heavy to pick up, so we've devised a technique to get you onto the truck. You need medical attention. As soon as we can maneuver you into the truck, you'll get what you need."

As Sara talked, Kate slipped around Pinkie and Sara and positioned herself on the porch of the house.

"Pinkie, we need for you to step onto the platform that Kate has made for you and face the truck. You need to hurry because you're losing a lot of blood," Sara said.

Amazingly and with no resistance, Pinkie stepped onto the platform and then turned and faced the truck.

Meanwhile, Ann had tied the second end of the rope to a tree limb, guided the second end through the pulley she had installed, and moved the knotted end so that it fell just below the back of Pinkie's head. She listened as Kate explained the procedure to Pinkie.

"Pinkie, we've devised a technique to get you onto the truck. We're going to secure a band underneath your armpits and gently guide you onto the truck," Kate said. As she talked, she was gently placing the knotted rope over Pinkie's head, and then she showed a thumbs-up to Ann, who immediately untied the first end of the rope, pulled it taut, and hurriedly retied it to the tree limb.

Seeing the rope was taut, Kate showed another thumbs-up to Ann, who climbed down from the roof and joined Sara and Kate, both of whom were now facing Pinkie at approximately ten feet.

"He can't use his right arm, so there's no reason to tie his hands," Kate said.

"Pinkie, you've been a disgrace to our civilization. You have killed innocent people; you have taken with malice money that belongs to others; you have no regard for the crushing agony you have caused innocent people. The justice system has been absent as far as you're concerned. Today, though, you'll reap what you've sown. You're standing on eight inches of ice, and you have a hangman's noose around your neck…"

Pinkie interrupted Sara in the middle of her dialogue and began yelling, swearing, and cursing. Large, ugly veins popped out in his face and neck.

Sara waited patiently until he ran out of steam and energy.

"So, at this moment and in the moments to follow, you have the opportunity to think about the path you've chosen in life and the grief you've caused innocent people. As the ice melts, the air you've breathed since you were born will be cut off, and you will perish. If you choose a quicker end to your fate, you can struggle to step off the platform we've made for you. I believe the better ending would be that you just allow the ice to melt, and you gradually feel your life melting with the ice. With that, we bid you goodbye."

With the conclusion of Sara's speech, the ice had melted slightly, and the rope had gotten tighter around Pinkie's neck. He again resumed cursing and swearing, but his outburst was tempered by the pressure on his throat.

After a few moments, Pinkie's facial expression softened. "Help me," he said. "Please help me. I never meant nobody harm. Please, please," he said, lifting his left arm slightly away from his body.

A few more minutes passed, and his words became garbled. Gurgling sounds began coming from his throat. His eyes enlarged to the point that they seemingly would pop out. The gurgling increased, and then his body relaxed remarkably.

Everyone waited until he expired.

"We'll take you to the hospital, dear," Kate said.

"Mother, I'll drive. Doctor Phillips will take care of me when I get to the hospital," Ann said.

CHAPTER 9

"Emergency Room," the sign read. It loomed just as prominently as Ann remembered, but its message shining red in the darkness caused it to have significant importance as a beacon to the sick and injured.

Parking several spaces from the Emergency Room door, she opened her car door, stepped out onto the concrete driveway, and immediately tumbled to the ground. "Ohhh! Ohhh!" she yelled.

A young man standing on the sidewalk several cars away saw her dilemma and rushed to the spot where she had fallen. Lights over the sidewalk lit up the area. Appearing dumbfounded at seeing a glamorous-looking young woman with red hair curled up on the pavement, he attempted to say something, but only mumbled sounds came from his mouth.

"Would you please help me?" Ann said, her voice distressed and pleading.

Still appearing baffled, the young man said, "Yes. Wha…wha…what…how can I help you, ma'am?"

"Please get a wheelchair and roll me through those doors up there," Ann said, pointing at the double doors that provided entrance into the emergency room.

"Okay. Okay," the man said and rushed away. Only a few seconds passed before he came running back with a wheelchair that swayed back and forth with his running.

"Help me get in it," Ann said, her face grimacing with every breath as she extended her hand.

The man jerked back as if he were being hustled.

"Please, please," Ann pleaded. "I can't get up without your help. My ankle's sprained or broken. That's why I can't get up."

The man hesitated for a moment, and then he took Ann's hand in his. "I may have to touch you…I mean, to get you up."

"Keep holding my hand, and then take your other arm and place it under my armpit. I'll grab your waist when you start to pull up," Ann said.

"You're sure it's okay?"

"I'm very sure. Look, I'm in a lotta pain, so please let's go," Ann said.

"Okay, okay, I'm gonna pull."

"What's your name?" Ann asked.

"Jimmy. My name's Jimmy."

"Okay, Jimmy, let's do this."

Jimmy slowly slid his arm under Ann's armpit. He was exerting a lot of caution to avoid touching anything other than her armpit.

"Pull, Jimmy, pull! Ohhh! Ohhh! Ohhh!" she yelled, and then Jimmy jerked her awkwardly into the chair.

"Let's go, Jimmy! Let's go! Push! Push hard! Get me through those doors!"

Jimmy grabbed the arms of the wheelchair and started pushing.

"Faster! Faster!" Ann yelled, and then she groaned loudly.

Jimmy accelerated his effort, and they arrived at the double doors in short order. He turned the wheelchair, pressed the automatic door opener, and then backed into the room.

A doctor walked quickly across the room and then stopped suddenly. He looked in the direction of Ann and Jimmy. "Well, Adventure Lady, or Ms. Patterson if we're on formal ground, has graced our presence once again. What brings you to my house this time?"

Ann looked at him for a moment, and then grimaced, "Ohhh, ohhh," she uttered. "It's my ankle. I think, uh, I think, uh, I do believe it's broken," she said and then grimaced again. Quickly evaluating her own statement, she said, "Well, it may not be broken, but it sure feels painful." Grimacing yet again, she added, "Let's put it this way. I can't walk on it."

"Who's your wheelchair operator?"

"Oh, that's Jimmy. I fell getting outta the car, and he was gracious enough to help," Ann said, and then she turned to Jimmy and said, "Thank you so much. Thank you."

"You're welcome. Do you need me anymore?"

"Jimmy, thank you for being a good caretaker for this woman. I'll take over from here."

"Okay," Jimmy said. He offered a small wave of his hand and walked away.

"Back to your ankle. Do you mind if the doctor looks at it and makes a prognosis?"

"Ohhh," she groaned loudly. "No, no, of course not, doctor," she answered quickly. "That's why…ohhh, ohhh, that's why I'm here." Here voice started strong and crisp but faded rapidly.

"I'm going to wheel you into a private room. I'll check you in. We should have a copy of your insurance card. After that, we'll take you down for an X-ray. I'll be just a moment to check you in," Doctor Phillips said.

Only a few moments passed before Doctor Phillips returned. "We're all set," he said.

Doctor Phillips had a slim build and stood one or two inches over six feet tall. He moved hurriedly with long strides. His high cheek bones caused him to appear to be smiling most of the time, and his fair skin with dark brown hair that was combed neatly to the left side created a striking appearance. He was nearing thirty years old, which is seen as young by most in his profession.

"Do you think it might be broken, doctor?" Ann asked.

"We'll do the X-ray first, and then I'll be able to let you know," Doctor Phillips said, and then he wheeled her into a private room. "I'm going to make arrangements for the X-ray," he said.

He was gone for only a few minutes before he rushed back into the room.

"Are you okay?" he asked Ann. "Well, I know you're not okay, but with the problem you have, are you tolerating the pain?"

"I'm doing better than expected," Ann said. "Thanks to your professional expertise, we may get this ol' ankle back in shape."

"Here comes your bed. The techs will get you situated, and off you go."

The techs supported Ann as she stood, and then they held her arms and helped her as she reclined on the bed.

"I'll see you in a few," the doctor said as the techs rolled her away.

It took several minutes to complete the X-ray, and then the techs rolled her back to her room.

"The doc will be here in a few minutes," one of the techs said.

"Do you want an extra pillow?" the second tech asked.

"Yes, please," Ann said.

Once Ann was situated and the techs were satisfied that it was okay for her to be left alone, they left the room.

Several minutes passed, and then the doctor entered the room. "Good news!" he said. "Your foot and ankle are not broken, but you have a nasty sprain. I'm going to have a tech come in and make a shoe for the foot. We don't want it to move whatsoever. So, you're confined to quarters for at least three days."

"Whatta you mean 'confined to quarters'?" Ann asked. "I only have a sprained ankle, and I need to go home."

"You need supervision, and I'm going to be the supervisor. I know we normally don't keep patients with a sprained ankle, but I'm making an exception in this case," Doctor Phillips said.

"I mean you're staying in this room for three days. We'll provide plenty of food and drink, and you can relax. With all your adventurous activities, you need a few days off doing nothing. Have you ever just done nothing? Have you ever just relaxed for a day or so?"

"Well, not in a hospital!" Ann said emphatically.

The doctor laughed. "We'll make it as comfortable as possible," he said. "I'll spend as much time with you as I can."

"Do you tell bedtime stories?" Ann asked.

The doctor laughed again. "I have a story of two young ladies on a barge. One of them decided to take a swim. She almost drowned. She survived only by the lucky chance of a dockworker being close enough to pluck her from the water. The next morning, she was found unconscious. She was rushed to the hospital, and I performed surgery on her pancreas. Remember?"

"Okay! Okay! No more bedtime stories! No more! No more!" Ann said loudly. "Yes, we were reckless. Yes, I should have stopped her. But I'm happy to report that Molly is going to school to become an attorney. Everything turned out okay."

The doctor looked at her for an uncomfortable length of time. His eyes were fixed on hers. Finally, he said, "I apologize. That was not an appropriate bedtime story."

"Accepted," Ann said quickly.

"Thank you. I'll leave you so you can get some rest. Is there anything I can get you?"

"No, I'm fine."

"I'll be back to check on you in a couple of hours. Meanwhile, I'll send someone from the kitchen to bring you some food. If you want a snack or a four-course meal, they'll get it. If you want a drink, they'll get that for you, also," Doctor Phillips said, and then his face broke into a broad smile. "Please use the call button if you need anything whatsoever."

"I will. Thank you, doctor."

"Please call me Noah. Yes, I know. My mother thought I'd be a good Samaritan if she named me Noah. So, I've been stuck with Noah from birth."

"I like it, Noah," Ann said, looking solemn then putting her hands to her face and smiling. She looked up and said, "Look at it this way. You graduated from saving animals to saving humans. Now, that's a noble cause."

"But you laughed," Noah said.

"Oh, I only laughed at your awkward manner in telling me your name."

"So, you're okay with my, uh, name?"

"Of course. Noah's a great name, Noah," Ann said.

"Great! On that note, I'll leave you for a few minutes, but I'll have food and drink delivered shortly."

Ann put her forefinger to the side of her head and said, "Didn't I hear the same statement about fifteen minutes ago?"

Noah laughed. "I believe you did. This time I'm gone."

After a few moments, an attendant came rushing into the room pushing a food cart that was loaded with different beverages, several kinds of pastries, boiled eggs, various fruits, a variety of deli meats, cheeses, and crackers.

"Is there anything else I can get for you?" the attendant asked.

Ann looked at the cart and then at the attendant. "I couldn't even imagine any other kind of food or drink," she said, her eyebrows raised so much that they nearly touched her hairline.

The attendant smiled broadly showing pearly white teeth and appeared pleased at Ann's statement. "Great! Please press your buzzer if you need anything at all. I mean, I'll get anything you need or want."

"Thank you. I'm good for now."

"I have a table for you," the attendant said. He positioned the table on the bed and placed several items of food on it. Moving the cart as close to the bed as possible, he let go of it and hurried out of the room.

"You know, I could use some whipped cream for the fruit," Ann said in a low voice. "Oh well, I'll make out with what I have." She looked at the table and smiled. "I'll have some fruit, a slice of chicken, a slice of cheese, and a cracker. I don't need pastries, and I don't need all those sugary drinks," she said as if talking to a food server.

She ate the food and drank a glass of distilled water. Leaning back on a pillow, she was amazed she felt no pain in her ankle. *That must have been a powerful shot,* she thought. *I may be able to get outta here in a day or two. I have so many things to do. I need to check on Mother and Grandmother to make sure they got away from Pinkie's okay. I need to know about our next assignment to catch the bad guys. With this ankle, I hope it's at least a week away.*

Continuing her thoughts, she felt she had deserted the produce company. *Dave will think I'm just not interested. I also need to go on the marketing trail. Why not start a new business that correlates with produce? Okay. What would that be? Maybe grow our own stuff? Yeah, that would be great! We could increase our bottom line or profit because our cost-of-sales should go lower. Nah, too many bugs, too many insects, and too much work and attention. Greenhouses? Now, that's a solution! Cover the thing with mesh fabric to keep the bugs out and let rainwater in. Yep! That's what I'll do. Start out with five or six and expand so that we're growing most of our stuff.*

She called Dave and told him she had personal things to do and would not see him for at least three days.

Lying back on the pillow, she closed her eyes and soon was in a deep sleep.

An hour or so passed before Doctor Phillips came rushing into the room. Seeing Ann was asleep, he stopped abruptly and began backing up.

"Noah, I'm awake. I heard this man come racing into my room and I thought there might be a fire somewhere."

Doctor Phillips laughed. "No, no, there's no fire. I've had a dozen things pop up, and I thought you might need something."

"No, I'm fine. Well, I could continue my nap."

"I'll leave you to nap."

Attempting to get comfortable, Ann rolled onto her right side and tried to relax.

Day two came, and Sara, Kate, Molly, and Cynthia visited her, and they had a pleasant visit. Ann told them she was going home the next day, and there was no need in them fighting traffic to come on the third day.

The days passed with a lot of bed rest, physical therapy, and watching people go up and down the hallway past her door.

At the end of the third day, Doctor Phillips walked rapidly into her room. "Ms. Patterson, would you accompany me for some green tea?" he asked.

"Doctor…Noah, you left me in this room for three days couped up like a chicken in captivity. Then you burst in and ask me if I would like some green tea. Here's what I want…freedom. I want a pink slip that reads, 'Ann Patterson, discharged.'"

Doctor Phillips's head dropped down quickly so that he was looking at the floor where he stood. After a few moments, he raised his head and looked at her. "What about a compromise?" he asked. "A pink discharge slip tomorrow morning at ten o'clock in exchange for a cup of green tea tonight?"

Ann's eyes instantly grew large, and a smile flashed across her face. "Noah, you have a deal!" she said, her voice loud and filled with enthusiasm. "What time is tea?"

Doctor Phillips stepped backwards, and he too smiled broadly. "You mean it? I mean…I mean…well, let's do it. Can you be ready in an hour?"

"I'm ready now, doc."

"Okay, okay. Here's the plan. You have to get outta here in a wheelchair. I mean, to be released you have to be rolled out. So, in one hour I'll arrange for an aide to come with a wheelchair and take you to the exit door. A large, black SUV will be waiting with a driver," the doctor said, and then he quickly added, "and, of course I'll be there also."

"Okay, let's get the show on the road," Ann said.

"I'll see you in one hour," Doctor Phillips said, and then he turned quickly and left the room.

An hour passed, and a tall woman wearing a white nurse's dress entered the room pushing a wheelchair. Her large-frame body sported large muscular-looking arms. "Ms. Patterson…"

"Yes."

"I'm here to take you to the exit door. May I help you into this chair?"

"Nah, I'm good," Ann said.

"Doctor's orders. I must help you."

"Okay, hold my shoulders, and I'll plop into your chair."

A faint smile crossed the woman's face, and then she said, "I gotcha."

"Good," Ann said, and then she sat down hard in the chair. "I'm ready."

"Very good," the nurse said. "Here we go." With that, the nurse expertly pushed the wheelchair out of the room, moved to the right side of the hallway, and proceeded at a fast clip.

Coming to a set of double doors, she said, "I'm gonna turn you around so we can get through these doors."

"Okay."

The nurse turned the wheelchair, backed up so her back touched the door, and then she pushed through.

"That was good," Ann said.

"We're here, Ms. Patterson. I'm to help you into the car." The nurse reached out and opened the door to the large vehicle. "I'm going to push down your footrest."

"Ready," Ann said.

The nurse pushed the footrest down with her foot. "Do you need my help to get you in the car?"

Ann looked at the nurse, and the nurse's head jerked back. Even in the darkness of the night, Ann's eyes were visibly sparkling. A smile flashed across her face. "I got it!" she said loudly. "I'm free! I'm free!" Holding the door open, she stepped into the vehicle and sat down.

"Hello, Ms. Patterson," a voice said.

"Is that you, Doc…I mean, Noah?"

"In the flesh."

"Sorry, my eyes haven't adjusted yet," Ann said.

"Is it okay to get started?"

"I'm ready."

"Good. We have a chauffeur. His name is Jake."

"Hi, Jake," Ann said.

"Hello, Ms. Patterson."

"Jake, we're ready," Doctor Phillips said.

"Everyone buckled up?" Jake asked.

"We're ready," Doctor Phillips repeated.

The vehicle moved forward.

"This green tea place is so close we could walk if we had the time," Doctor Phillips said.

"I have all night," Ann said, "but I have to be back in the hospital by ten in the morning so I can officially get discharged."

Doctor Phillips laughed. "You drive a hard bargain, Ms. Patterson."

"I just make sure that promises made to me are kept," Ann said, "especially those made by doctors."

Doctor Phillips laughed. "We're here," he said.

They went into the restaurant and had two cups of tea each as they talked about where they worked. After forty-five minutes, Doctor Phillips asked, "Do you like the symphony?"

"I've never been," Ann said.

"You haven't been?" Doctor Phillips asked with an astonished tone. "Well, one of the seventies bands is appearing with the symphony. Would you consider accompanying me tomorrow night?"

"Tomorrow night? I'll be celebrating my freedom tomorrow night, but hey, why not. Can you get tickets that fast?" Ann asked.

"I'm a doctor. I have special privileges," Doctor Phillips said, and then he laughed. "Just joking, but I do have a way to get tickets."

"Okay, where do we meet?" Ann asked.

"Is it okay if I pick you up at your home?" Doctor Phillips asked.

"What if I meet you just outside the Emergency Room?" Ann said.

"That'll work. There's a restaurant just across the street from the symphony. Would you consider having dinner before we go to the symphony?"

Ann hesitated for a moment but finally said, "Sure. What time should I be at the hospital?"

"Great! Great!" Doctor Phillips said. "Okay, six o'clock. Park down at the end of the Emergency Room driveway. Jake will drive us again. We'll be sitting there waiting for you."

Ann was released from the hospital the next morning wearing a boot on her left foot and spent the day with her mother and grandmother. Later that day, she drove to the hospital and met Doctor Phillips.

"How was your first day of freedom?" Doctor Phillips asked.

"I spent the entire day with my mother and grandmother. It was nice just being with them."

"I think I told you I ate at your mother's restaurant."

"I'm not sure that you did," Ann said. "At least, I don't remember it."

Doctor Phillips made small talk primarily about eating at Kate's café until they arrived at the restaurant, went in and were seated, and then placed their order for their dinner. He again started talking about Kate's café. "If this is a sore spot, please cut me off," he said.

"Oh, I will, and the name of the café is Sara's Kitchen," Ann said.

"Oh, right, it is. The mayor had a heart attack and died at the café, didn't he?" Doctor Phillips asked.

"He did," Ann said.

"Did that hurt your mother's business?"

"Not really. No one liked the mayor anyway. There was little sentiment from the customers."

"Did your mother go to the pokey because of that?"

"No, she went to prison because she knocked off a man who was beating the hell outta her."

"Oh," Doctor Phillips said, and then he appeared puzzled at what to say next.

"It's okay," Ann said. "It's difficult for people that never has problems in their life to understand the actions of a person that does have problems. For a person to understand, they have to experience trauma in their own lives."

"I agree totally," Doctor Phillips said. "I see that often in my work. So many people lack the fortitude to stand up for themselves. Some do, and I think that's admirable." He paused for a moment and then asked, "Do you mind if I ask how your mother fared in the, uh, the place where she had to go?"

"Nashville Women's Prison," Ann said.

"Oh."

"It's perfectly okay to say she was in prison. She has no qualms about talking about her experience," Ann said.

"That's remarkable. Some people lock the experience away in their minds to forget it, which is the wrong thing to do. How did she fare?"

"She experienced the depths of hell; she was thrown into the hole; the guards beat her. The warden noticed her, though," Ann said.

"How so?" Doctor Phillips asked.

"She was and still is a beautiful woman. The warden saw her and arranged for her to stay in an apartment just doors away from his office. She didn't share the room; she had a kitchen, she had a TV, she had it all except for one thing."

"What was that? Well, I have a hunch what it was," Doctor Phillips said.

"What do you think?" Ann asked.

"Uh, well, uh, she was called on for favors."

"She was forced to have sex with the warden over and over. I am a product of those encounters."

"Oh," Doctor Phillips said, sounding apologetic.

"That's right. My mother had to endure the despicable acts of that animal."

"Where is he now?" Doctor Phillips asked.

"He's dead."

"Oh."

"He was invited to be a guest of the president of the United States along with several other persons, and he was allowed to take my mother. At the end of the day, all the guests had dinner with the president. Fortunately, the warden had a heart attack during the dinner and fell dead on the table."

"Oh, my gosh!" Doctor Phillips said loudly.

"It caused quite a stir," Ann said.

"I can only imagine," Doctor Phillips said. "Our food is here. I hate that. Now we have to eat rather than talk. I enjoyed talking with you so much. You have an incredibly unique way of expressing yourself."

"Thank you…I think."

They ate and then attended the symphony. Jake drove them back to the hospital and then dropped Ann off at her car. She got in and drove to her mother's house.

It was getting close to midnight, but Ann walked to the front door, knocked, and announced loudly that it was she that was calling at that time of night.

Dressed in a nightgown, her mother opened the door. "Honey, is anything wrong?" Kate asked, her voice sounding a tone of alarm.

"No, no, Mother. I just came by to talk. Is that okay?"

"Of course, it's okay. You're sure there's nothing wrong? How's your ankle?"

"I did, Mother, and it's fine. I just have something to share with you."

"Okay. Okay. Do you want something to drink?"

"A glass of water would be nice," Ann said.

"I'll be right back. We can sit in the living room and chat as long as you want," Kate said, and then she hurried to the kitchen and returned with two glasses of water. "Here you are, honey," she said, handing Ann a glass of water. "What's bothering you, honey?"

"Well, uh, do you remember when Molly and I went to the hospital? Molly was very sick. Remember?"

"Of course, I remember. You met a young doctor there…wait, wait, you're not about to talk about the doctor, are you? You're sure about the ankle?"

"The ankle's fine, Mother, and yes, it's about the doctor. I had tea with him last night, and we went to the symphony tonight."

"Oh, my."

"Mother, my body felt funny when I was with him. I don't know how to describe it. I work with Dave, but I never think about him being other than just Dave. The doctor, though, is something else. I just feel odd."

"Honey, I fully understand. As a young woman, I had several encounters, but they never worked out. You see, your grandmother Sara and you and I are different from other people. We demand respect, and when it doesn't happen, we take actions that other people don't. We don't think about it; we don't question it; we just act. I'm afraid that's what would happen with your doctor."

"You really think so?"

"Yes, honey. Like I said, we're different; we react differently; we solve things in our own way," Kate said.

"What should I do?"

"I can only tell you what I would do if I were faced with the same circumstances."

"What?"

"To avoid some grim fate that might befall the doctor, I would cut it off. I would gracefully back off and go on with my life."

"That drastic?"

"Yes, honey. It's the only way."

Ann looked away from her mother and stared into space for what seemed like several minutes. "Okay, Mother. I agree. I will call the doctor tomorrow and let him know. After that, I think I'll fly down to Miami and then drive to Key West for a few days."

"All by yourself, honey?"

"Yes, Mother. I'll check in with Dave, but I'll call you every day. I've never had a vacation. It might be good for me."

Kate stood up, walked hurriedly to Ann and embraced her. It was an unusual act because none of the women showed compassion or feelings although they possessed a profound degree of thought about the security of each other.

The next day, Ann made a reservation at a Key West Airbnb, and then she called Doctor Phillips and told him that she would not see him any longer. She did not know how to interpret his silence on the other end of the telephone, so she ended her part of the call.

Her thoughts immediately changed to her trip, so she packed a suitcase, drove to the airport, signed up for a standby flight, and waited until a flight was available. To take care of responsibilities and to kill time, she called Dave to let him know she would be gone for a week. After that, she called her grandmother and mother and talked with them about the job they had just completed and the prospect of a future job.

Three hours passed before she was called for a flight. She eagerly boarded the plane, took a window seat, and waited.

CHAPTER 10

The flight to Miami was one of frustration because an overzealous man sat beside her and continually tried talking with her and touching her with his elbow to get her attention. She thought about snuffing him out but reminded herself they were on an airplane, and her act might not be looked upon favorably. So she moved to a vacant seat at the back of the plane and fumed because she was not able to silence the irritating man.

When the plane landed, she waited until she could hide herself in a group of people that were disembarking. When they reached the jetway, the group of people separated, and Ann was forced to walk alone. She did not want to encounter the man who had upset her.

Exiting the jetway, she joined another crowd of people and breathed a sigh of relief because the man was nowhere in sight. Following the signage, she went to a rental car station, rented a car, and was soon on her way to Key West.

As she drove, her thoughts flashed from one subject to another. She did observe the unusual environment, though. During part of the drive, she could see water on both sides of the highway. Being unfamiliar with the surroundings, everything was strange to her because she had not taken the time to research the environment. She passed a sign that read "Overseas Highway." The drive reminded her of the time she spent on the bank of the Cumberland River. It was there that she cultivated her awareness of the environment and the beauty that Mother Nature produces.

Continuing her drive, she became aware that the area between the highway and the ocean served as a buffer and that in itself was enticing. The beauty of the area was overwhelming, and she was most impressed with its primitive look.

The drive proved to be longer than she expected, but finally she arrived at Key West. Using the GPS on her telephone, she arrived at her destination, a bed-and-breakfast facility, in a brief period of time. It was a huge Victorian-style building that was situated only a few hundred feet from the Gulf of Mexico. She smiled. "I need a room where I can see the water," she said in a low voice.

She parked, retrieved her suitcase, went inside, and was immediately greeted by a host, Mrs. Russell, a pudgy woman with a wide, contagious smile. At full height, she came only to Ann's shoulder.

"Welcome to 'Russell's Home Away from Home.' We promise a great night's sleep," Mrs. Russell said. "Are you Ms. Patterson?"

"I am. I'm happy to be here. Do you have a room overlooking the water?" Ann asked.

"Most certainly. We have a room just for you with a to-die-for view. We have free wi-fi; we have books in your room; we have a great breakfast for you; we've done everything possible to make your visit the most wonderful experience possible."

"Everything sounds perfect. As we agreed, I will be here through Friday and check out Saturday. Is that still okay?"

"Yes, Ms. Patterson. You will have five fabulous nights with us."

"Is it possible to go for a walk along the water?" Ann asked.

"Well, there's a bluff just below, and it winds around for several hundred yards. Once you leave our home, there's no civilization for a quarter of a mile. I would not advise going for a walk by yourself. It's too desolate, and you're too pretty to be out by yourself."

"Thank you. I'll just enjoy the water from the front porch. Would you recommend a restaurant for lunch and dinner?"

"Of course. I'll write some restaurant names and addresses on a sheet of paper. Just give me a minute."

"What about sightseeing? What would you recommend?"

"Well, you must visit Ernest Hemingway's residence. What a man and what a writer! Now, if you don't like cats, you might give the visit a second thought because there are many cats living there."

"Cats are okay," Ann said.

"And chickens. They are a protected species here. They walk through the restaurants, especially through seafood restaurants along the water," Mrs. Russell said.

"Well, I'll just have to live with the chickens," Ann said.

"Are you here on business, Ms. Patterson—if I may be so bold to ask?" Mrs. Russell asked.

"No, I'm just taking a few days off," Ann said.

"What do you do for a living?" Mrs. Russell asked.

"I own a produce company in Nashville."

"Oh, how thrilling! Is that Tennessee?" Mrs. Russell asked.

"Yes, Nashville, Tennessee, Home of country music."

"Oh, I love country music! Dolly Parton, what a lovely woman! What a wonderful singer!"

Ann smiled. "Well, I think I'll freshen up and go out for dinner," Ann said.

"Oh, oh, let me get you the names," Mrs. Russell said. She stepped into an office behind the reception desk.

Ann waited.

Mrs. Russell returned in a few moments holding a sheet of paper. "Here you are. There are three seafood restaurants, two American-style food, and an Italian restaurant. They are great! I hope you enjoy."

"I'm sure they will be great. Would you mind showing me to my room?" Ann said.

"Of course. Follow me."

Ann picked up her suitcase and followed Mrs. Russell, who opened the door for her.

"This room is decorated as if it got stuck in the Victorian Age. The floors have been cleaned; the sheets have been washed and disinfected as well as the pillows; the entire room has seen the greatest degree of attention just for your visit," Mrs. Russell said.

"It's fabulous," Ann said. "I will be incredibly happy here. Thank you for giving it so much attention."

Mrs. Russell smiled. "Please let me know if you need anything."

"I will. I'll see you in the morning for breakfast," Ann said.

"Sharply at seven. We have a wonderful breakfast, and we don't want it to get cold," Mrs. Russell said.

"I'll be there."

Mrs. Russell closed the door.

"Whew," Ann sighed. "I need to call grandmother and mother." Pulling her phone from her purse, she dialed her mother's number.

"Honey, are you okay?" her mother said, her words rushing and sounding concerned.

"Yes, Mother. I'm fine. I just had a long session with the proprietor of the bed-and-breakfast. Her name's Mrs. Russell. The name of the B&B is 'Russell's Home Away from Home.' She's so concerned that I'll be happy and have anything I want."

"That's wonderful, honey. How was the flight and drive down to Key West?" Kate asked.

"I had some difficulty on the flight. A man sat next to me and harassed me so much that I moved to the back of the plane."

"Oh, honey! Did you correct him?" Kate asked.

"No, I was on an airplane, Mother. I had to sit there and do nothing."

"I'm sorry. What about the drive down?" Kate asked.

"At the start of the drive, I was so preoccupied with the plane ride and with Doctor Phillips that I wasn't too attentive with the drive. As I drove, though, I began noticing the beauty of the environment. I would look around and see water on both sides of the highway, and that was great too."

"Will you promise me you'll have a good time?" Kate said.

"I'll try. I'm going to call grandmother, and I'll call you tomorrow."

"All right, honey. Goodnight."

"Goodnight, Mother," Ann said, and then she hung up and called Grandmother Sara.

After that, she relaxed on the bed which was so soft that her body practically sunk in the stuffing of the mattress. "Too soft," she said, "but hey, I'm at home away from home so just live with it."

Ann closed her eyes and told herself that everything was okay, and it was time to relax.

After some time, she checked her phone and was shocked that it had only been thirty minutes since she first laid down on the bed. "Dinner," she said. She freshened up and called for a ride to a seafood restaurant she had selected earlier. The restaurant was open on three sides, giving the sense of eating on a covered outdoor patio. Once seated, she studied the menu and ordered the seafood special. Just as Mrs. Russell had told her, a chicken with five small chicks came marching through the restaurant. Because she was in the produce business where products had to be as clean as possible, she questioned the practice of allowing chickens so much freedom around food.

An employee came by and asked if everything was okay. Ann remarked that the food was delicious, paid her tab, and then called for a ride and returned to her room. She used her phone to set an alarm for five-thirty in the morning.

The next morning, she got ready and arrived at the breakfast table at five minutes before seven. Four other couples were seated, all of them appearing to be sixty years of age or older. She took a deep breath and thought the age difference was fortunate because they wouldn't want her tagging along, and she would not have to blend into their agenda.

"Good morning," the couples all said in unison.

"Good morning," Ann said and forced a fake smile.

"How was your night, dear?" one woman said.

"I slept like a baby," Ann said.

"How delightful," another woman said.

Ann didn't respond but ate quickly and called for a ride to Ernest Hemingway's former residence. Once there, she immediately observed how stately the structure stood with its subdued yellow façade. It had two stories with a pleasant, lighted interior.

"Would you like to tour the residence?" a woman asked.

"I am very interested in seeing the residence," Ann said.

"Very well then. I'm not busy at the present, so would you object if I gave you a VIP tour?"

"I would be honored," Ann said.

For the next ninety minutes, Ann followed the woman and listened as Hemingway's life was narrated.

"Every morning, Mr. Hemingway would go to his studio and write for the entire morning," the tour guide said. "He enjoyed the mornings because of the quietness. Afterwards, at noon, he would visit his favorite tavern, drink, and trade stories with the locals."

"Fascinating," Ann said. "What is the story about the cats?"

"That is most interesting, and I'm gratified that you noticed the cats. They have free reign of the house. You noticed one sleeping on the bed. There are approximately sixty cats domiciled here, and they are all polydactyl; that is, they are all six-toed. The usual toes for a cat are five in the front and four in the back."

"Remarkable!" Ann said. "I'm so happy I was able to visit this residence."

"I am most happy you enjoyed it," the woman said. "May I show you anything else…perhaps take you to the gift shop?"

"Yes, I would be delighted to visit the shop," Ann said.

The woman led Ann to the gift shop where she browsed for several minutes before buying two books. Thinking about her mother and grandmother, she bought each of them a book, and then she called for a ride and instructed the driver to take her to another seafood restaurant. She decided she would try a different one every day she was in Key West.

When they reached their destination, Ann paid the driver and got out of the car.

"Hey, lady, wanna go for a ride on a jet ski?" a man yelled from a nearby boat.

"No, thank you," Ann said, and then she smiled. *It might be fun,* she thought, *but I'm not ready for it just yet.*

She went into the restaurant, which again was open on three sides. The fourth side had a solid front which led to the kitchen.

After ordering the luncheon seafood special, she settled back with a cold glass of tea. It was very pleasant just sitting out in the open air near the water, watching the boats coming and going.

"Well, hello again," a voice said.

Ann jerked around and came face to face with the man who had harassed her on the airplane.

"Is this seat taken?" the man asked. Without waiting for an answer, he sat down in a chair that was directly across the table from her.

"I came here to be alone," Ann said.

"Oh, testy, testy. All I wanna do is to talk to you. I'll even buy your lunch," the man said.

"No, thanks," Ann said.

"What are you having?" he asked. "By the way, my name's Robert. My friends call me Bob, but I go by Robert or Bob. It don't matter to me. Say, what is a beautiful woman doing eatin' by herself?"

Ann sipped her tea and looked at the man.

"You're not very talkative, are you?" Robert said.

"Ma'am, is this gentleman with you?" a restaurant employee asked.

Ann hesitated for a moment then replied, "Actually, he is."

Robert jerked back in his chair. "Now, that's the spirit! After lunch, why don't we go to my room and spend the afternoon?"

"Are you married?" Ann asked.

"Well, yeah, but what does that matter?" Robert said.

"Actually, I'd rather take a walk alongside the water," Ann said.

"Now, that sounds great! Where do we go?"

"What about tomorrow morning, but you'll get lost until then so that I can have my lunch," Ann said.

"Sounds like a deal. Where do we go?" Robert asked again.

"There's a nice place to walk about two hundred feet from Russell's Home Away from Home. It's a bed-and-breakfast," Ann said.

"Where's that?" Robert asked.

"If you're interested, you'll find out. Be there at five-thirty in the morning.

"Five-thirty! It's dark then," Robert said.

"You wanted to walk. There's nothing like taking a long, cool walk in the morning," Ann said.

"Whoa! Sounds better and better," Robert said. "I'll be there! I'll see you tomorrow morning." He rose, lifted a hand in farewell, then left Ann to eat alone.

Although Ann's meal was served quickly, she was so agitated by Robert's visit that all she thought about was leaving the restaurant. She took a few bites, paid the check, and walked to the boardwalk that bordered the pier. *Smells like fish,* she thought, and then she decided she should explore the area that overlooked the bluff. She should know what was on the other side of the piece of land that was about a hundred feet to the left of an imaginary straight line from Russell's bed-and-breakfast.

Calling for a ride, her spirits suddenly lifted. The ride came and delivered her to Russell's bed-and-breakfast. She paid the tab, got out, and walked down to the edge of the bluff. Huge rocks lay along the edge of the water. Waves splashed powerfully along the base of the bluff and then receded, only to repeat the process repeatedly.

She smiled at the choice of the location and reminded herself that she needed a pair of leather gloves that were one hundred percent clean…so clean that not even the smallest, microscopic fiber rested on the gloves. She had a pair of gloves in her purse, but she was concerned it could be possible that the gloves picked up a small piece of fiber inside her purse.

Suddenly, she slapped her forehead with an open hand. "A fatal mistake! A fatal mistake!" she huffed, irritated with herself. "My footprints are all over the ground." She thought for a moment. *Well, I'll just have to walk at an angle and make sure that I'm a couple of hundred feet away from here. I need a lint remover and a box of booties.*

Having decided what she needed, she called for a ride and instructed the driver to take her to the first seafood restaurant she had visited. From there, she walked to a strip mall she had noticed the day before and went inside a drug store. It had a self-checkout register, and she thought everything was falling into place. She bought a lint remover, brush, a box of booties, and a box of quart-sized plastic bags. After checking herself out, she called for a ride.

Suddenly, a large box truck with lettering on the side that read "Shred Truck" rumbled past her. She observed it casually just as she observed other vehicles speeding past her. Suddenly, she stopped and thought for a moment, and then she started running after the truck. "Whoa!" she yelled as she ran onto the street chasing the truck. "Whoa!" she yelled again. "Stop the truck! Stop the truck! Stop, stop, stop!" she yelled. A car passed her and pulled in front of her which blocked her view of the shred truck. "You!" she yelled. "Why did you do that? Why did you do that?" she shrieked.

Continuing to run, she didn't notice that, all at once, she was parallel to the truck which had pulled over to the curb and stopped.

"Hey, lady!" the driver of the truck yelled.

Ann powered down her running until she came to a stop and looked in the direction of the truck driver yelling. Her eyes enlarged and sparkled in the sunlight. "It's you," she said slowly as she panted for breath. Taking a moment to recover from the run, she walked to the shred truck.

"Were you yelling for me?" the man said loudly.

"I was. I was," Ann said, her breath coming hard. "I have some documents to shred," she said. "They're not wrapped up, but I can do that tonight."

"Do you have an account with us?" the driver asked.

"No, no, I don't have an account with you…well, yes, I do. I do…not in this city but another city."

"Okay, so what's your question, lady?"

"I want to throw documents in your truck to shred…tomorrow. Where will you be tomorrow?"

"I'll be right where I am now. I've not worked this street yet."

"You'll be here tomorrow? You really will! Good! Good! That is, well, is it okay if I throw just an envelope of documents in with all your other documents to shred? Do it tomorrow?"

"Sure, lady. I'll be in this spot at ten in the morning."

"You will? I mean, that's great! I'll be here way before ten just waiting on you. You're sure you'll be right here on this spot tomorrow?"

"I'll be here, lady."

"I'll see you tomorrow," Ann said, her eyes sparkling with a glow enveloping her face.

The shred truck pulled away, and Ann got a ride back to the bed-and-breakfast. *I'm prepared*, she thought. *I'm completely prepared.*

Once inside the bed-and-breakfast, she was met by Mrs. Russell.

"Oh, my, my, my," Mrs. Russell said. "You look so nice. Do you have time for a question?"

"Of course."

"Do you like chicken salad?" Mrs. Russell asked.

"It's one of my favorite foods," Ann said.

"Oh, my, my. Would you like a chicken salad sandwich with an apple?"

"I would love it," Ann said.

"I'm having one too. Would you like to join me?"

"I'd be delighted," Ann said. "I bought some items. Let me take these to my room, and I'll be right back."

"I'll wait for you," Mrs. Russell said.

Ann took the items to her room, put them in her suitcase, locked it, and returned to eat with Mrs. Russell. When they finished, she went to her room and thought about the next morning. She would wear four sets of booties. The ground to the bluffs was mostly gravel with many larger rocks which created an irregular pattern for walking.

As she thought about getting to the bluffs, she suddenly remembered the bicycles that were available for guests. Weighing the risks of taking a bike, she couldn't think of anything that would create a problem, so she decided to take a bike and ride to the left side of the property rather than going straight to the bluffs. At some point, she would put down the bike and walk to her right to meet Robert. The key to her plan would be that she would have to avoid being seen both coming and going by the guests at the bed-and-breakfast.

After planning her meeting in the morning, she showered, watched TV, set her phone alarm for four in the morning, and then turned in for the night to sleep.

Four o'clock came early, but she hopped out of bed, freshened up, put on jeans and a silk blouse. Next, she pulled four pairs of booties over her shoes, stuck the leather gloves in her jeans pocket, and eased out the door of her room. Being extra careful not to make noise, she slipped out the front door, put on the leather gloves, got a bicycle, and began peddling to the left side of the property just as she had decided the night before. The darkness was more of a problem than she had anticipated, but a full moon provided enough light to see the bluff. The darkness, however, was beginning to give way to light, and the morning began to be filled with gray light.

Deciding to leave the bike, she dismounted and began walking to her right several feet away from the bluff. As she walked, she began looking for the perfect place to meet Robert. The morning light was beginning to take hold, and she could easily see the edge of the bluff and the water as it crashed against the rocky bottom at the base of the bluff.

"Hello there," a voice said.

Ann turned quickly to look. "You're early," she said.

"Wanted to make sure I was here in case you showed up. Oops, wait a minute. My phone," Robert said.

As Robert was occupied with his phone, Ann hurriedly checked her leather gloves and pulled them tight. *The phone*, she thought. *I must get his phone.*

"Okay, it was just my wife. I told her I was busy and not to bother me," Robert said.

Ann looked at him as the muscles in her face tightened. "Bob, I was just looking down at the water and how it splashes in and then splashes out. Isn't it beautiful what Mother Nature has done?"

"Just what are you looking at?" Bob asked.

"Down there. Let me hold your phone and take a peek over the edge there and look at the beauty."

He gave his phone to Ann and said, "Well, let me look. Man, I have a beautiful woman here, and I'm looking at water."

"Bob, you have to get closer to look. Are you afraid you're gonna fall?"

"No, I ain't afraid," Bob said with an irritable voice.

"Well, if you're not chicken, then step up there so you can see the beauty of the water," Ann said.

"Okay, okay, I'm up to the edge now."

Without any emotion and holding his phone in one hand, she closed her hands to make fists, placed them on Bob's shoulders, and gave him a firm push. He didn't scream; he didn't make any noise; he simply plunged headfirst toward the rocks below. It seemed an interminable amount of time passed before his body crashed into the rocks. He resembled a blob that had been carelessly tossed down the side of a cliff. His head dangled at an irregular angle away from his body, and his arms appeared as noodles lying on the rocks.

Standing erect, she threw Bob's telephone as far as she could into the churning water.

She backed away from the cliff and walked back to the bike. She got on and peddled at a moderate rate to the bed-and-breakfast, parked the bike, took off her gloves, and then slipped into the house. Walking as softly as she could, she went to her room, opened the door as quietly as possible, and went inside. "Breakfast in forty-five minutes," she said in a faint voice.

She took a quick shower, checked her cosmetics, changed clothes, placed her gloves and booties in a brown envelope, and then joined the other guests for breakfast.

"Good morning," one older woman said. "How was your night?"

"Quite peaceful. I slept like a baby," Ann said.

"It must be nice," the woman said. "George and I are up three or four times a night. If it's not one of us hurting, it's the other. Maybe entering the golden years is not what it's cracked up to be."

"Perhaps it'll get better," Ann said.

The woman looked at Ann with a puzzled expression, then said, "I hope you're right."

Ann finished her meal and then watched TV in the lobby for an hour before going to her room to get the brown envelope. She then called for a ride, which came in a short time, and she directed the driver to take her to the street where the shred truck was supposed to be. Arriving thirty minutes early, she got out of the vehicle and sat down on one of many benches that lined the sidewalk.

Thirty minutes passed, and a truck horn sounded from the street. Ann looked up to see the truck and then propelled herself off the bench. "It's me! It's me!" she yelled.

The truck pulled to the curb, and the driver got out and met Ann. "You made it," he said.

"I made it," Ann said. "Where do I throw my package?"

"I'll open the door. It's at the back of the truck. You can just toss it in," the driver said.

"And then it'll be shredded?" Ann asked.

"Into tiny strips that even a magician couldn't put back together."

"One of the documents is in a long piece of plastic," Ann said. "It's pretty thick and hard plastic."

"Good as gone," the driver said.

Ann looked at the driver for a moment. "Okay, there it goes," she said, tossing the envelope as far as she could.

The driver shut the door and turned on the shredder. "Nothing escapes the shredder," he said.

"Amazing! Isn't technology just great!" Ann said loudly and cheerfully.

"Technology's changing the world," the driver said, his voice sounding as if he were a great statesperson.

Ann laughed. "Thank you so much. You are a great asset to Key West."

"Thank you, ma'am. All accolades accepted."

"Good day and thank you again."

The driver went back to his truck, climbed in, and drove away.

Ann went back to the bench and sat down. *Why do I feel so down?* she thought. *I ate breakfast, so I should feel okay. I do need to call Dave a little later though.*

"Good morning," a voice said.

Being preoccupied, Ann didn't answer.

"Dear, are you worried about something?" the voice asked.

Suddenly realizing that someone was near her, Ann jerked. "Oh, oh, I'm sorry. I didn't see you sit down."

"Oh, my, my, me. It's nothing to worry your little head about. I just saw you looking as if you have lost your best friend, so I thought I'd sit down and try to cheer you up."

"Uh, okay, oh, I'm not, uh, I mean I'm not upset about anything. I'm fine, as a matter of fact."

"Now, that's good to hear. My name's Gladys, and I bet I can guess your name…"

Ann turned quickly to look at her. Her eyes grew large as she gazed intently at Gladys. "Now, how in the world would you know my name?"

"Oh, my dear, Gladys gets around. I'm telling you she does."

"Okay, I'll bite. What's my name?"

Gladys smiled. "Okay, let's see. If I remember correctly, your mother's name is Kate…"

"What!" Ann said loudly. "How did you know that? How did you know my mother?"

"Oh, my, my, I've eaten at her restaurant many times as well as your grandmother, Sara."

"Wha…what! You know my grandmother?"

"Oh, most certainly. Actually, I know her better than I know your mother."

"And my name?"

"Why, Ann, of course. You were the cutest baby in the whole wide world, and then you turned beautiful. Now, you're still beautiful," Gladys said.

Ann gazed at her a moment before saying, "Well, I must tell you that I'm impressed. How did you know my name? I've never owned a restaurant, nor have I ever owned anything where you could just walk in and entertain yourself."

"Oh, honey! I have so many sources at my disposal. I couldn't begin to remember which one told me your name. You must admit that I'm good, aren't I?"

"I agree with that," Ann said.

"So, tell me why you look so gloomy?" Gladys asked.

Ann hesitated and then she said, "I'm not like other people, nor are my mother and grandmother. We don't think like other people; we don't react to circumstances like other people; we go against the norm many times."

Gladys put her hand on Ann's shoulder. "Is it okay if I put my hand on your shoulder, dear?"

Ann's eyes focused on Gladys's eyes and remained there for several moments, and then she said, "I suppose so…well, yes, of course it's okay." She turned to look away from Gladys and think about their conversation.

"Honey, I know you and your family like I know the back of my hand. Of course, you're different. Wouldn't it be sad if everyone was the same…thought the same? Stand up with your shoulders straight and be proud you're different. Never, never question your differences with other people. They are the ones that should worry. Do you understand what I'm saying?" Gladys asked.

"Well, yes, I believe I do. At least I feel better. In fact, I feel really good, and it's all because of you."

"One last thing. All of you watch your backs," Gladys said.

"Gladys," Ann said, and then she turned to look at Gladys, but the bench where Gladys sat was empty.

"Gladys, Gladys!" Ann cried, jumping up to look around the bench and in the different directions away from the bench. She thought about what had just happened. "Well, that was weird," she said.

Ann returned to the bed-and-breakfast, watched TV, and wrote in detail about her meeting with Gladys. She knew she had to share the meeting with Sara and Kate as soon as she got home.

The next day, she had breakfast, paid the rental bill for staying with Mrs. Russell, drove to the airport, and flew back to Nashville.

CHAPTER 11

The return flight to Nashville was unusually smooth, and Ann informed the pilot that it was an extremely comfortable flight. She exited the plane and boarded the bus which took her to the parking area where she got her car and drove to Kate's home. She was anxious to talk about her meeting with Gladys.

Exiting the car, she grabbed the paper detailing her meeting with Gladys and rushed up the porch steps. Just as she reached the top of the steps, Kate opened the door.

"Honey, why the hurry?" Kate asked, her voice sounding concerned.

"Mother, we need Grandmother here! I have a dynamite story!"

"You do? Oh, you want me to call Grandmother?" Kate asked.

"Yes, yes, please."

"I'm calling now," Kate said.

"Good. I'll get some tea for everyone," Ann said.

A few moments passed, and then Sara and Kate joined Ann.

"Honey, you have a big story. What's going on?" Sara asked.

"Grandmother, you will not believe what I'm about to share with you and Mother. Do you want some honey in your tea?"

"Please."

Ann gave Sara and Kate each a glass of tea and then unfolded the record of her meeting with Gladys. Because she had written in detail the entirety of the meeting, she was able to recite every aspect of her conversation with Gladys.

Sara sat back in her chair and appeared to be in shock. She drew herself back to the table and said, "Honey, my grandmother's name was Gladys. She's been deceased for twenty or twenty-five years, but Gladys was her name. Can you describe her?"

"Absolutely. Her hair was dark blonde, and she had a round face. And, oh, she had a very small scar on her cheekbone close to her left ear, and, and her eyes were the lightest blue I've ever seen!"

"Honey, that was your great-great-grandmother. There's no doubt about it, and that's scary. Gladys came back to tell us something. We just have to figure it out. Okay, she said to watch our backs. How do you interpret that?"

"Well, it means someone has us under surveillance and means to do us harm," Kate said.

"But who?" Ann asked.

"Honey, you know we're on the bad guys' list. That part of the population has their own means of communication, and without a doubt, they have communicated about our remedying the ones we have been assigned."

"Grandmother, this is another subject. Have we been assigned or contacted about remedying any other bad guy?"

"Not yet, but I believe the next assignment is to be a woman," Sara said.

"That'll be different," Ann said.

"Changing back to Gladys, we need to find out if there are any clues as to why Gladys showed up," Kate said.

"Grandmother, where did Gladys live, or maybe the most important, where did she die?" Ann asked.

"She lived in a small town named Loyston in East Tennessee," Sara said.

"Loyston?" Ann said. "That's an odd name."

"It was named after John Loy, who settled his family there around 1800," Sara said.

"Wow! What a history lesson that would make," Ann said.

"There's more," Sara said. "The Tennessee Valley Authority, known as TVA, made plans in the early 1930s to build Norris Dam, which is a few miles north of Knoxville. So, they forced all the people who owned land along the river that was to be dammed to sell it to the TVA. Now, most of the people wouldn't sell, so TVA took it by eminent domain. All the business owners lost their businesses.

"Gladys and Grandfather George owned a small grocery store. George would travel to Knoxville to buy flour, sugar, and other staples. They also sold produce which was furnished by local farmers. They barely made a living; they worked night and day; they saw it all disappear when Norris Dam was complete, and the Clinch River covered their store, their home, and all the dreams and memories that had been accumulated during their lives."

"That's terrible," Ann said, "to see your possessions and memories covered by water just because the government decided to do it."

"That's what happened," Sara said. "The people who lost their homes had to move, of course, and that included Gladys and George. They mostly located to nearby communities of Knoxville, Clinton, and Rocky Top which used to be called Lake City. Gladys and George moved to a small community north of Knoxville. Their children were grown by now and moved away from that area. The trauma of losing everything they had caused friction in their marriage, and they divorced. Gladys worked in a grocery store until she died. She did not have a rewarding life. Just before she died, she asked her pastor to make sure she was returned to a cemetery near what used to be Loyston. That's where she rests today," Sara said.

"But we don't know if she still rests there," Ann said.

"What do you mean?" Kate said.

"I mean we need to find out if she's still in the cemetery," Ann said.

"Of course, she is, honey. She's been resting there for many, many years," Sara said.

"Well, we need to find out. Mother, will you go with me?" Ann said.

"To where?" Kate asked.

"To the area around what used to be Loyston."

"Of course, I'll go with you. I'll go with you wherever you wanna go."

"Great! So—" Ann said, her statement interrupted.

"But we don't know where to go or how to get there," Kate said.

"Give me a minute. I'll check information on my phone," Ann said.

A few moments passed as Ann studied on her phone. "Okay," she said. "Here's the scoop. Like you say, Grandmother, Loyston is under water. No road that I see goes to that area. There's a state park north of Knoxville that has a trail to an area called Loyston Overlook. Along that trail is an old cemetery. I'll be willing to bet that's where Gladys is resting."

"Or not resting," Kate said.

"Kate, what a thought coming out of your mouth!" Sara said.

"Well, Ann saw something, Mother," Kate said.

"Grandmother, will you please give us your blessing if Mother and I just go snooping around where Gladys rests?" Ann said.

"Of course, you have my blessing. You just have to promise to be careful," Sara said.

"Yes! Be careful, we will! We're off, Mother," Ann said.

"Let's leave at seven in the morning, dear," Kate said.

"I'll pick you up at seven," Ann said. "I'm going home. It's been a long day."

Everyone said goodbye, and Ann left for home.

The next morning, Ann drove to Kate's home and arrived sharply at seven o'clock. Kate was waiting and got into the car.

"Good morning, sweetheart," Kate said.

"Good morning, Mother. Are you ready for this adventure?" Ann said.

"I am. Do you have our route all planned out?"

"I do. We're driving to Knoxville first," she said as she began to drive. "That'll take about two and a half hours, so we'll stop for a break… maybe Crossville. After we get through Knoxville, we have about a twenty-minute ride on the interstate and then about fifteen minutes on a state road."

"That's perfectly okay, honey. I'll just be a quiet passenger and let you do all the hard work," Kate said.

Ann laughed. "Sounds good," she said.

Nearly four hours passed before they pulled off the highway and parked.

"We're here, Mother. Are you okay?"

"I'm fine, dear. What's next?"

"There's a trail nearby that goes by an old cemetery. I'm betting Gladys will be resting right on that plot of ground."

"Let's go then," Kate said.

They got out of the car and began walking along a trail that was flanked on both sides by trees that looked as if they were touching the sky.

"What beauty! This is absolutely paradise!" Ann said loudly. "Mother, look, look at the red bushes and the yellow bushes that are brushing up against those gigantic trees that are sweeping the clouds! Have you ever seen anything as magnificent as this?"

Kate laughed. "Honey, it's like the wilderness has made a giant bouquet for us to enjoy."

Just then, a man and a woman approached them from the opposite direction.

"Good morning," Ann said.

The man and woman smiled and returned the greeting.

"May I ask you a question?" Ann said.

"Sure. Go ahead," the man said.

"Do you know where the town of Loyston used to be?" Ann asked.

"Absolutely. There's an overlook about a mile down the trail. Just look down at the water, and you'll be looking at where Loyston used to be," the man said.

"Wonderful! What about an old cemetery?" Ann asked.

"Stay on this trail. It's about halfway to the overlook. It's a little off the trail, but you'll see it easily," the man said.

"May I ask you another question?" Ann said.

Kate laughed. "This is my daughter. She's full of questions."

The woman with the man laughed.

The man looked at the woman for a moment and then said, "Oh, it's quite all right. Young people should be curious," he said, and then he smiled.

"Are all the graves old?" Ann asked.

Both the man and woman smiled.

"Yeah, honey, they're old. They're real old…well, except for one. It's fresh. We believe what happened, though, is that lightning hit a tree and knocked it over on a grave and damaged it. We think the Park Service relocated the grave."

"Of course, they did!" Ann said, her voice bubbling with excitement. "Would you know…I mean, would you just happen to know if the tombstone…there was a tombstone, wasn't there?" she said, her voice now cracking with emotion.

The man and woman now looked at Ann with puzzled expressions.

Apparently seeing their expressions, Ann said, "Oh, please, please, let me explain. We're looking for my great-great-grandmother's grave. Her name was Gladys. We believe she's buried in the old cemetery."

The expressions on the couple's faces relaxed.

"Well, good luck with seeing the names. That's a real old cemetery," the woman said.

"I'm sorry we took—or I took—so much of your time, but thank you so much," Ann said.

"It was a pleasure," the man said.

The woman smiled, took the man's hand, and they walked casually away.

"Mother, Mother, we're gonna find her," Ann said.

"It sure looks promising," Kate said.

They walked for a few minutes until they came to a hilltop that overlooked a valley filled with trees adorned with yellow and red leaves. Pines large and small dotted the landscape.

"What a beautiful vista," Kate said.

"Mother, can you imagine Gladys living here? She was surrounded by all this beauty, and to have it jerked right from beneath her is the greatest injustice that anyone can imagine," Ann said.

"It's beautiful, dear, but times were hard back then. I doubt if Gladys even noticed nature's beauty very much except maybe a look or two in the spring and one in the fall," Kate said.

"Well, that's terrible. I wish I could have reminded her of the beauty of Mother Nature," Ann said.

Kate laughed. "Honey, we have to start looking for the cemetery."

"There! There! Just beyond the clump of trees. See!" Ann said with excitement as she began to walk faster.

Once they were at the cemetery, Kate said, "This is one really old cemetery."

"Look, Mother, there's the fresh grave, and it does have a tombstone," Ann said, and then she ran to the grave.

"See the 'G,' Mother. The other letters are faint, but that's Gladys right there. We're going to have to exhume her, Mother. We have to find out how long she's been dead."

"Exhume her! We're in a state park, Ann. We can't exhume a grave."

"Of course we can, Mother. I'll bring half a dozen of the guys from the shop, and we'll get it done in just a few minutes. We'll be in and outta here before you can blink your eyes."

"No. N…O. We're not touching this spot; we're not exhuming; we're letting Gladys rest just where she is. Besides that, we don't even know if that's Gladys," Kate said.

"Okay, Mother. Now, we'll never know."

"Let's go, honey. It's a long drive back," Kate said as she began walking away from the cemetery.

"Okay, you know best," Ann said, and then she hurried to catch up to Kate, who was already a few yards away.

"Let's go to the overlook and then go home," Kate said.

After looking down from the overlook, they walked back to the car and started home. Four hours later, Ann pulled alongside the curb at Sara's home.

"We have to report to Grandmother," Ann said.

"Of course, we do. Mother's gonna laugh at us for making the trip in the first place, but she gave her blessing for us to go," Kate said.

"Do you think if we acted like dummies, it'd be okay?" Ann asked.

Kate laughed.

They got out of the car, went to the front door, and Kate rang the doorbell. The door opened, and Sara smiled. "It's the ghost hunters," she said with a pleasant voice.

Kate patted Ann on the shoulder and said, "I told you so."

"Let's go in and take our medicine," Ann said. Once inside and seated, Ann said to Kate, "Well, am I going to tell the story, or are you?"

"The floor's yours," Kate said.

Ann looked at her grandmother, took a deep breath, and started speaking slowly. "Well, we saw where Loyston used to be. There's an overlook that looks right down in a valley where Loyston once was."

"And the cemetery?" Kate said.

"Oh, yes, the cemetery. Yes, we found a cemetery with a fresh grave. A man on the trail told us he thinks lightning hit a tree and damaged a grave which was relocated. We found it…"

"And…" Kate said.

"And…and, it had a tombstone with the letter G on it. The other letters were worn by the weather, but I sincerely believe it was Gladys."

"So, you have nothing to show for your trip except sores on your butts?" Sara said.

Kate looked at Ann who returned the look.

"That about sums it up," Kate agreed.

"Well, Kate, you know better, but you both learned a lesson. I didn't object to your going because I wanted both of you to experience something or remind yourselves of what I'm about to tell you.

"We're in a very dangerous business. There are bad people who play games on vulnerable people. Ann, you went to Florida with a heavy load on your shoulders. You were susceptible to being taken advantage of…oh, the door. I'll be right back."

A brief time later, Sara returned with Molly at her side. "Look who has come to visit us," Sara said.

Ann jumped up and ran to Molly. "Girl, I haven't seen you in a month of Sundays. You remember my mother, Kate?" she said and laughed.

"Of course, I've seen your mother. I've seen her more times than you've seen me," Molly said. "Some of us work; some of us study for school; some of us go to Florida and play."

Kate and Sara laughed.

"Now, that says all you wanna hear," Molly said.

"Well, I'll just skip right over the comedy stuff. Have we graduated yet?" Ann asked.

"No, I'm working on it though. I've been studying down by the river where we used to live, but I'm getting hassled by some guy I don't even know."

"What'd you mean you're hassled?" Kate asked.

"Well, this guy comes by and gets really close and asks me what I'm doing. I don't give him the pleasure of responding, but he is persistent. Then he asks me if I'll come up to his room."

"What do you do then?" Kate asked.

"I tell him to leave me alone, but that doesn't seem to help," Molly said.

"Whatta you think we should do about that, honey?" Kate said, looking at Ann.

"We're experienced at handling such situations as that," Ann said.

"That we are," Kate said.

"Whatta you think about us peepin' in?" Ann said. "Maybe just be standing behind a tree when Mr. Uninvited Guest shows up."

Kate smiled. "I like it," she said.

"Now, you girls have to be careful. That's outta our jurisdiction," Sara said.

"Mother, you taught us everything we know," Kate said. "Of course, we'll be careful."

"You really don't hafta to do this," Molly said. "I'll just study somewhere else."

"Molly, Molly, we don't run just because someone is a bad guy. No, we're trained by my mother to take care of business," Kate said.

"Okay, when do we start this little expedition?" Ann asked.

"Nothing like the present," Kate said. "Let's suit up and be there about an hour before dark."

"Sounds like a plan," Ann said.

"Molly, do you go in by the church?" Kate asked.

"Yes, ma'am," Molly said.

"How many feet down the path do you go?"

"All the way to the riverbank," Molly said.

"Okay, we'll be there about five-thirty. You show up around a quarter of five, sit where you usually sit. We'll watch for you to come by the church, and then we'll station ourselves out of sight at the riverbank."

"What gear are we taking?" Ann asked.

"Carry your nine-millimeter," Kate said. "You just never know when it comes to activities like this."

"What about the pulley?" Ann asked.

"Good idea!" Kate said in a loud voice, smiling from ear to ear. "I have it, and I have rope. I'll throw those in the car."

"You have the canvas bag?" Ann asked.

"I do, and I'll throw the items in it. I hope we don't go down the trail clinking like a machine shop," Kate said.

"Okay, girl, we're gonna solve this little problem. You won't be bothered after tonight," Ann said.

"You won't do anything bad to him, will you?" Molly said.

Ann put her hands on each of Molly's shoulders. "Molly, we're teachers. We teach bad guys not to be bad. That's our calling in this life."

"That's a very nice way of putting it," Kate said.

CHAPTER 12

The meeting at Sara's home ended around forty minutes after Kate and Ann arrived to tell Sara about their trip to find Loyston. After that, everyone went their separate ways to prepare for the anticipated showdown on the riverbank that afternoon.

Arriving at her home, Ann pulled on a bullet-proof vest, red plaid shirt, jeans, and leather boots. She checked the clip in the nine-millimeter and then shoved it in a holster which she strapped to her waist with a black leather belt. So that the holster and revolver would be covered, she chose a lightweight jacket that was long enough to fall just below the holster. Completing her dress, she donned a black baseball cap with white letters on the bill that read "BGMD." It was an anacronym that stood for "Bad Guys Must Disappear."

After she had finished dressing, she recovered the vehicle keys from her pants that she had been wearing, driver's license, a twenty-dollar bill, and then she left to go to Kate's home.

Only a few minutes later, she pulled in front of the house. Getting out of the car, she checked her appearance reflected in the car window. Satisfied, she walked up to Kate's front door and knocked. Only a few moments passed, and the door opened.

"You look ready for business, honey," Kate said.

"Thank you, Mother. Do you need help with anything?"

"No, I'm ready. Would you like a chicken salad sandwich before we go?" Kate asked.

"I would, and a glass of tea," Ann said.

"Come in and sit at the table, honey."

Ann went into the kitchen and sat down at a corner table that had two chairs. "We need something to carry the pulley," she said.

"I have two zip-up canvas bags, one with the pulley and the other one for the rope. I told you I was ready," Kate said. "Here's your sandwich." She slid the plate with the sandwich to Ann.

"Thanks. You're my mother. How could I ever think that you would not be prepared?"

Kate laughed. "You're good for your mother's morale, honey."

Ann smiled. "Good sandwich," she said. "We need to park as close to the church as possible to avoid suspicion from any cop that may be waltzing by."

"We've always had good luck in that department," Kate said. She hesitated a moment before adding, "Except for that one time I had to go to the pokey. That was my fault. I was so angry and filled with contempt that I just foolishly left a place with so many clues."

"I'll watch after you, Mother," Ann said.

Kate laughed. "Eat that last bite and let's go, honey."

Ann ate the remainder of her sandwich, drank some tea, and got up from the table. "I'm ready," she said.

"I'll drive unless you have an objection," Kate said.

"Perfectly okay," Ann said.

They picked up their packages, left Kate's house, got in the car, and Kate drove them to First Avenue on the east side of the city.

"There's our spot," Ann said. "Someone was so nice to leave that parking spot for us."

"I told you we live under special stars," Kate said.

They parked, got their bags, and walked to the church.

"Oh, my gosh! They have hot dogs," Ann shrieked. "That was a standard staple on the church table when Molly and I lived on the riverbank. They put it out for the homeless people."

"Well, get one if you're still hungry," Kate said.

"No, I'm full of my mother's treat. Want a bottle of water?" Ann asked.

"I do."

Ann got a bottle of water for Kate and one for herself, and then they walked to the end of the path and to the edge of the embankment that overlooked the river.

"It's almost five o'clock," Ann said.

"We're on schedule. Which tree do you want?" Kate asked, pointing to a tree to her left and then one to her right.

"I'll take the one on the right. Let's not shoot each other," Ann said.

"No doubt we'll move toward our subject," Kate said. "If and when we do, I'll text you and let you know which way I'm going. There's so much noise down here that no one will hear the ding of the phone. We must try to synchronize our movement if at all possible."

"After all this preparation, it'll be terrible if the subject is a no-show," Ann said.

"Please don't think that way, honey. Remember, we're under special stars."

"You got it," Ann said. "Ready to take our posts?"

"Let's go," Kate said. "See you in a few."

Each of them took their posts and waited.

After a few moments, Molly appeared, pulled out two books from a backpack, sat down on a rock, and opened one of the books.

Ann received a text from her mother that read, "She's early!"

Ann acknowledged the text.

They both continued to wait. At five-fifteen, a stocky man who appeared to be a few inches short of six feet tall strolled into view. He had a thick, dark beard but appeared to be in his twenties. He immediately went to Molly.

Ann received another text that read: "I'm going to work around and come up behind him. You try to do the same on your side."

"Will do," Ann replied.

Both had to traverse tall strands of weeds to reach the path that would allow them to come up behind the man that was now occupied with Molly.

Only a few moments passed, and Kate and Ann met on the path. They each removed their revolver from its holster and walked on tiptoes until they reached the area where Molly was seated. The man stood looking down at her.

Kate stuck the barrel of her revolver to the man's neck. He immediately turned to see who was interrupting his progress with Molly. Ann immediately stuck the barrel of her revolver to the opposite side of his neck. His movement stopped.

"Is this man bothering you, ma'am?" Ann asked Molly.

Molly hesitated for a moment, and then she said, "He's repeatedly asking me to go to his room, but he said if I don't go voluntarily, he'll physically take me up."

"My, my, my. You're a bad guy, mister," Kate said. "Now, I'll warn you. You move again, and you'll lose your head." Speaking loudly to Ann, she said, "You ready to release some lead?"

"Ready," Ann said. "Molly, get your books and go up the path but not far enough that you're out of sight of us."

Molly grabbed her books and stood up quickly. Her face was distorted, and her legs trembled. She staggered to stand beside Kate. "Can I stand here for a minute?" she asked.

"Of course, you can. You can stay here for two minutes, three minutes, or whatever suits your fancy," Kate said.

"You women playin' cops and robbers?" the man asked.

"We're not playin', scumbag. We're goin' to put you off the street, and that'll be one less scumbag for society to worry about," Ann said.

"I don' believe ya," the man said and began to turn.

Just as quickly, Ann thrust her foot into the back of his kneecap, causing him to bend over and then sink to the ground.

Kate followed him down with her revolver held against his head. She moved behind him so he couldn't reach her leg and pull her to the ground.

Ann motioned for Molly to follow her a distance away from the man.

Molly looked confused, but she followed.

When they were out of earshot of the man, Ann said, "Scumbags like this have to be taken off the streets. No man has a right to abuse women, especially you. Just think about how far you've come. You've pulled yourself up from living on the street; you've adopted great habits; you've set yourself on a course to be a great attorney. My grandmother, Sara, has a lotta resources, and she cares for you just as if you were her daughter. You've got the world in the palm of your hand. Fight evil, girl. That's what it's about. Fight evil.

"Now, this scumbag is going to get punished, and my mother and I are going to do it. What we need from you is to watch out for anyone that might stumble in here for some unknown reason. Do you think you can do that for us?"

Molly raised her head slowly and looked at Ann. Even though darkness had blanketed the area, lights from town and spotlights from across the river provided enough light for Molly and Ann to see each other.

"You are my best friend," Molly said, her words coming slowly and deliberately. "You've helped me change my life." Again, the words came slowly, but this time they sounded as if she were reaching into the very depths of her heart and declaring that she was so blessed that someone had come along that cared for her. "Of course, I'll watch. If anybody comes along, I'll come runnin."

"Great! Here's your speech lesson for the day: Instead of saying 'If anybody comes along…say 'If anyone comes along.' Doesn't that sound a lot better?"

Molly smiled. "It does. Thank you. When I'm by myself and dark comes, I move up to the church. They have lights, and it's safer."

"Okay, I'll be back. Keep your eyes open."

"Yes, ma'am."

Ann returned to join Kate. "How's the scumbag?"

"He's still here. I think we should hook him up to the pulley and lower him into the river and let him rest there for ten or fifteen minutes. Whatta you think?"

"You ain't goin' to lower nobody," the man said loudly and then jerked upwards.

Ann slammed her foot into his back, causing him to fall back to the ground.

Kate picked up a hand-sized rock and threw it against the back side of the man's head. "Let's get to it," she said.

"The party boat comes right past here," Ann said. "If it does, we need to drop him really fast." Looking up at a tree that grew a few feet from where the man lay, she said, "I need to climb that tree and anchor the pulley right above where that big limb comes off the trunk. I can tie the rope around my waist and pull it up as I go up."

"Can you see good enough?" Kate asked.

"Oh yeah, no problem."

"What about falling? Will you be okay?"

"Mother, you worry too much. I can climb as good as any animal in the forest, and I'm an expert with a pulley."

Suddenly, the man sprang up, pushed Kate to the side, and started to run.

Just as quickly, Ann held her leg and foot out, causing the man to stumble and crash forward onto the ground. The force of the movement caused her to fall backwards against the tree, but she maintained her balance and stood upright.

"Are you all right?" Kate said, rushing to her.

"Yeah, I'm fine, but scumbag's not. He met the ground with his face pretty hard."

"Well, let's get this done," Kate said.

Ann tied the rope around her waist, grabbed the pulley, and approached the tree. As she did, an unidentified boat with two bright lights passed very close to where she, Kate, and the man were located.

"Down! Get down on the ground!" she yelled, and then she fell to the ground and positioned herself in a prone position. Once down, she looked up at the path but didn't see Molly. She then looked toward Kate and the man on the ground. *Everything looks good*, she thought.

"Is the scumbag moving?" she asked Kate in a loud enough voice that Kate would hear.

"He's out cold," Kate said.

Ann crawled to be close to Kate. "It's going to be difficult to pull this off at this location," she said.

"I totally agree. Any ideas?" Kate said.

Ann hesitated for a moment, and then she said, "What about leaving him in Tent City?"

"A fine idea!" Kate said. "How do we get him there?"

"Well, we surely have to wake him. If we had a bucket of water, we could just douse him good. No one's going down to the river to get water though," Ann said, and then she rubbed her forehead and looked out into the darkness. Suddenly, she tossed both arms above her head. "The church! The church has bottles of water on their food table all the time. I could use my telephone flashlight to find the way up the path. Would you be okay if I left Molly and you with our guest?"

"Of course," Kate said.

"Will you keep your revolver trained on his head while I'm gone?" Ann asked.

"I will indeed, my dear daughter. Now hit the road, or in this case, the path," Kate responded.

"Okay, okay, let me bring Molly down here." Ann went up the path to where Molly still hugged the ground. "Molly, it's okay now," she said. "You can get up now."

Molly didn't move for a moment. Finally, she raised herself so that she rested on her knees and, after another pause, she stood upright.

"You okay?" Ann asked.

"I'm fine. What's goin' on?" Molly asked.

"Will you come down and join Kate?" Ann asked.

"I'm right behin' ya," Molly said.

They walked to join Kate.

"He hasn't moved yet," Kate said.

"Okay. Molly, I'm going up to the church to get some water to pour on him. Will you stay with Mother and make sure our guest doesn't wake up and run away?"

"Sure. We'll watch him like a hawk," Molly said.

Ann smiled. "Great! I'll be back quickly." She turned and started running up the path. She had walked the path so many times that the flashlight was hardly necessary, but it enabled her to go faster. Once she emerged from the woodsy area and entered the manicured grounds where the church displayed their food table, she was pleased to see six bottles of water on the food table. She stuck a bottle in each of her jeans' pockets and then took two bottles of water in each hand and ran back to join Kate.

"Any change?" Ann asked Kate.

"He's still out like a rock," Kate said.

"You okay, Molly?" Ann asked.

"Just fine."

"Okay, we have a favor to ask of you. We want to walk this scumbag to Tent City and turn him over to them. You know most of the people there. Would you talk to them and ask them to take our guest off our hands?" Ann asked.

"Of course. When do we go?" Molly said.

"Just as soon as we get him awake," Ann said as she tipped a bottle of water over his face.

He didn't move.

"He gets a double dose," Ann said, and then she emptied another bottle.

"Uh, uh, wha…" the man grunted.

"Get up," Ann said. "We're going for a walk."

The man looked up, revealing his bloody face.

"Take your shirt off and wipe your face," Ann said.

The man groaned and grunted for a few moments and then rose to his knees.

"Take your shirt off and wipe your face," Ann repeated.

The man continued to groan, but he slowly pulled his T-shirt over his head and just as slowly wiped his face.

"Get up," Ann said. "We're going for a walk. Is everyone ready?"

"Let's do it," Kate said.

"Molly, you stay ahead of us and do the talking."

"Yes, ma'am," Molly said.

After a few moments, the man got to his feet, and the procession started toward Tent City with Ann and Kate holding their weapons at the back of their captive. The trail paralleled the river and would have been too difficult to see except for the various lights that came from the city. The usual fifteen-minute walk turned into twenty-five minutes, but they finally reached their destination. Molly ran ahead and talked to a man who was joined by other men in short order. She ran back to join the procession.

"They're ready to take him," Molly said.

"Good." Ann pressed her revolver into the man's back. "We're going to talk with these people," she told him.

The procession moved to within a short number of feet of the men Molly had met, and then Ann, Kate, and Molly backed away, leaving the man with the inhabitants of Tent City.

"Let's go home," Kate said.

"Yeah, I'm for that," Ann said. "We have to stop and get our equipment though," she added.

"I'm happy we're going," Molly said.

CHAPTER 13

Two days after the scene at the riverfront, Kate and Ann were summoned by Sara for an urgent meeting. Ann rushed to Sara's house and met Kate on the steps to the front door.

"Do you think we're in hot water again?" Ann said.

"We're going to find out very soon," Kate said. "Do you want to go in first or shall I—"

The door suddenly opened before Kate could finish her sentence. "Welcome, my sweet children," Sara said.

"Oh my," Ann said in a hushed voice.

"I have tea for all, and I have your favorite chairs just waiting. Please come in. Molly beat everyone, and she is already seated," Sara said.

Ann looked at Kate, who had an "Oh my gosh" look on her face. Ann couldn't hold back a snicker.

"Come in. Come in," Sara said. "Would you like one of my famous sandwiches made with my secret recipe?"

"Mother, which would be a chicken salad sandwich," Kate said as she and Ann walked into the house and took their seats in the living room.

"But, of course," Sara said. "It was handed down by my mother."

Ann glanced at Kate. "Of course, I'll take one," she said.

"Me too," Kate said. "We would be remiss if we didn't have one of your famous recipe sandwiches."

"You're trying to be funny, I'm sure," Sara said.

Ann laughed, and then Kate joined in.

"Now, now, isn't that pleasant," Sara said, and then she got the sandwiches, returned to the living room, and gave Kate and Ann each a sandwich. "When everyone is comfortable, I have a very important matter to discuss."

"We're ready, Mother," Kate said.

"Ladies, we have been successful in apprehending two very bad men. No longer will those two misfits perpetrate any harm to society. Now, we're ready to start a new assignment. Allow me to refresh your memory. Our new adventure is Sally Sue Cross Bottoms. She was a mother of three. Two of the children were drowned by her in the family's bathtub. She filled the tub with water, dragged the two youngest children to the tub, forced them in the water, and then held their heads underwater until they perished. Once she was finished, she went upstairs and suffocated her ten-year-old daughter as she was peacefully sleeping.

"As the children lay dead where they perished, Sally Sue waited patiently until her husband came home from work as a heavy equipment operator. She held a double-barrel shotgun on him, then escorted him through the house and showed off her handiwork with the children. When she finished with the tour, she blew his head off with the shotgun. The rumor was that he was having an affair with his boss's wife. Everything she did was recorded on the home security cameras. When she finished with her grisly deeds, she disappeared.

"The legal enforcement community has looked for Sally Sue for five years. She has been extraordinary in her elusiveness. Only infrequently have tips led the legal community to locations where she was reportedly residing. None of those tips led to anything, or Sally Sue had fled the scene.

"Oh, but there's more! It seems Sally Sue has been spotted around nightclubs in Nashville. The word is that she makes a living as a call girl and a stripper. She rips off foolish old men who are conned by her into believing they are special. A girl has to make a living, you know."

Everyone laughed at Sara's unusual sense of humor.

"So, we're going to take the obvious approach to introducing ourselves to Sally Sue by hanging around the nightclubs. We have an old picture of her, but she has surely changed her appearance by now, and Mother Nature has helped also. There's one telltale physical item about her, though. Her left hand was burned severely somewhere along the line, and all the outer layer of her skin was burned off. Only the second layer exists, and it is pale and white-looking. Naturally, we're going to zoom in on any woman that possesses such a hand. Are there any questions?" Sara asked.

There was silence for a moment, and then Ann asked, "When do we start?"

"How about tomorrow night?" Sara said.

"Sounds fine to me," Kate said.

Ann and Molly agreed tomorrow night would be great.

"Good!" Sara nodded. "Shall we all meet at Kate's house tomorrow at seven o'clock and every night thereafter until we narrow down the nightclubs that we should concentrate on?"

"Am I invited?" Molly asked.

"Honey, this may turn out to be a time-consuming affair and a wild goose chase on top of that. I think it would be to your advantage to stay home and study your schoolwork," Sara said.

"Yes, ma'am," Molly said, her voice low and sounding hurt and dejected.

"There's one more thing we must do before we adjourn, and that is to vote. I will vote first, Kate next, and Ann last," Sara said.

After they voted, Sara counted and recorded the vote. There were two black marbles and one white. Sara announced the vote and reminded everyone that Sally Sue's punishment would be at the discretion of the person or persons that apprehended her.

"Anything before the meeting's adjourned?" Sara said.

"Not for me," Ann said.

"I'm good," Kate said.

"Good. The meeting's adjourned," Sara said. "See everyone at Kate's home at seven tomorrow night."

"I suggest we pack our nine-millimeters," Ann said.

"Of course," Sara agreed.

With that, everyone went their separate ways.

The next day passed without incident, and everyone met at Kate's house at seven o'clock as planned.

"I have a shoulder holster," Ann said. "If I get in a squabble, I'm not going to be fiddling around in my purse for my weapon."

"That's a good idea," Kate said. "I have mine in a side holster, and I'll be just as quick as you are."

"Mother, you're always trying to be a step ahead of me, but you're never going to make it."

"Ladies, ladies, we're on the same team," Sara chided, and then she smiled. "A little competition is never lost in the wind," she said in a soft voice.

"How're we going to approach this?" Ann asked.

"I think we should split up," Kate said. "That way we'll cover more ground."

"Advice accepted," Sara said. "Kate, you and Ann take one side of the street, and I'll take the other," Sara said.

"That'll leave you all alone, Mother," Kate said.

"I'll be perfectly fine," Sara said. "Let's start at First Avenue and work our way up to Bridgestone Arena. If any one of us spots Sally Sue, text everyone with the word, 'Spot,' and then send the address in as brief a text as possible. Don't any one of us approach Sally Sue without backup. We'll meet at the corner of Fifth Avenue at Bridgestone Arena. Text when you're there. Any questions?"

"I have none," Kate said.

"Nor do I," Ann said.

"Then let's go apprehend a criminal," Sara said.

"Are we riding together?" Ann asked.

"Certainly," Sara said. "Only one car makes good sense. We'll try to find a parking spot on First Avenue, and then we'll start our journey."

Ann drove everyone into the city, and then she parked on First Avenue.

"I'll take the south side of the street," Sara said. "We need to circulate in each club as much as possible, so I'm thinking we'll spend at least thirty minutes in each place. The clubs with two or more floors will take longer, of course. Ladies, it's going to be a long night, but let's go."

"Please be careful, Mother," Kate said.

"Yes, please, Grandmother," Ann added.

"Sssh, don't worry about me. I'll meet you at Bridgestone."

Sara crossed over to the south side of Broadway and started walking in a westerly direction. Kate and Ann began walking in the same direction but on the north side of Broadway.

Six hours passed, and Kate and Ann crossed Broadway to meet Sara. Much to their dismay, she was not on the corner, nor could she be seen on any sidewalk.

"Now, where is she?" Kate asked.

"Don't worry, Mother. You know how thorough Grandmother is with everything she does. She may have latched onto something."

"Why don't I call her?" Kate said.

"Now, that's an idea," Ann said.

Kate began punching numbers on her telephone.

"You ladies waiting on someone?" a voice said.

"Grandmother!" Ann said in a loud voice and then ran to meet her. "It's you. We were worried that someone had taken you home with them," Ann said.

"Oh, no, no! I'd scratch their eyes out if that happened. Besides, I have a friend in my pocket that shoots loudly and packs quite a wallop. No one saw anything interesting?" Sara said.

"No, even though we did a lotta walkin' and heard a lotta talkin,'" Ann said. "Well, shall we go home and do the same thing tomorrow?"

"We shall," Sara said. "Let's get rolling."

The women walked back to First Avenue and climbed into Ann's car. She drove to Sara's house first and dropped off her grandmother, then she went on to Kate's. "See you at seven tomorrow night," Ann said.

Kate bade her goodnight, and Ann drove home, took a shower, and went to bed.

Getting up the next morning was a task for Ann because she hadn't slept soundly. She dressed, had a cup of coffee, and drove to the produce company where she met with Dave. He assured her that all operations had been operating smoothly. In fact, he had added three large accounts for customers.

For the next six hours, Ann called the new customers as well as some of the large companies that had been with her for several years. Feeling relieved, she drove home, had a cold glass of tea, a submarine sandwich, took a shower, and then drove to Kate's for their nightly meeting.

Once the meeting was called, Sara once again gave instructions. "Let's do the same thing we did last night but shift sides. I'll take the north side, and you and your mother take the south side," she said and looked at Ann.

"That okay with you, Mother?" Ann said, looking at her mother.

"Fine with me," Kate said.

Ann drove everyone to First Avenue, and they got out of the car and started walking to their new assignment.

Kate and Ann's first stop was a two-story club. They surveyed the first floor, and then took the elevator to the second floor.

"You realize she could be taking the elevator down while we're going up," Kate said.

"I thought the same thing, Mother. Why don't I go back down and watch the traffic from the elevator while you survey the second floor?"

"Good idea. I'll see you downstairs," Kate said.

After a few moments, Kate joined Ann on the first floor. "See anything?" she asked.

"Nothing. Let's proceed," Ann said.

After several stops, and in particular the clubs with two and three floors, Kate said, "No wonder Mother was late last night. She had more stops than we did, and some of the stops have several floors."

"You're right about that, Mother. She had more faces and arms to look at," Ann said.

After several more stops and seven hours later, Kate and Ann arrived at their meeting spot at the arena. Sara was not at the meeting place.

"She can't be late again," Kate said, "unless she's on to something."

"Why don't we give her another fifteen or twenty minutes and then go look for her," Ann said.

"That's a plan," Kate said.

Ann checked the time repeatedly on her phone, and then she said, "Mother, let's go look for her. It's been twenty-two minutes already."

"Let's get going," Kate said, and then she looked at Ann. "Don't worry about Mother. She's a tough old bird, and she can take care of herself."

"Let's still look," Ann said, and with that, they crossed the street and began looking at buildings on the north side of Broadway.

After several calls to Sara and checking every club as they neared First Street, Ann said, "Mother, these clubs are closing, and I don't know how much longer I can be on this bad ankle."

"Honey, we lack two buildings. Please try to work with it until we finish."

"Of course, Mother."

They finished their search mission at three in the morning. There wasn't any way that Sara could have gotten by them, and besides that, Sara knew the owners and managers of the clubs. They certainly would have helped her if she had run up against foul play.

"What do we do?" Kate asked. "We surely just can't go home and pretend that nothing happened."

"Let's stay until sunrise," Ann said. "By that time, she may have escaped from whatever is holding her, or one of her friends took her home."

"But she would have called us," Kate said.

"Yes, you're right. Well, let's go home now and freshen up, and then come back and leave no stone unturned," Ann said.

"Done. Pick me up at ten," Kate said.

"Should we file a missing person report?" Ann said.

"We can't afford to get the cops involved," Kate said. "Too much explaining to everyone."

The next morning, Ann was waiting in Kate's driveway at ten minutes before ten.

Kate opened the front door of her home and gave a thumbs-up signal to let Ann know she was on her way. A few moments later, two sedans came by slowly, hesitating first at the rear panel of Ann's vehicle and then at Kate's house. Their windows were heavily tinted, making it impossible to see how many people were inside, let alone who they were.

A few moments passed, and Kate came to Ann's vehicle and got in.

"Mother, we have visitors," Ann said, and then she started driving toward the city.

"Where?" Kate asked.

"Two dark-colored sedans just passed. What do you want to bet they are tied to Sally Sue in some way."

"Why do you think that?" Kate asked.

"They drove slowly either taking pictures or getting your address… probably both," Ann said, "and they did a rolling stop just before they passed me…no doubt to get my license plate number!"

"Sally Sue may have more contacts than we know about," Kate said.

"With her alleged night jobs, she just may be better equipped than we know," Ann said.

"That presents a very serious problem," Kate said.

"If you're thinking what I'm thinking, how do we protect our homes while we're scouting around Broadway?" Ann said.

"Exactly," Kate said.

"Well, let's look for Grandmother, and at the end of every hour, let's come back and check on our homes," Ann said.

"That's a lotta running, but it's probably necessary. It's something we have to do," Kate said. "We'll be spinning our wheels on both fronts…looking for Mother on the one hand and rushing home to check on our homes that have been sitting there for an hour without protection."

"Good point. Our homes have alarm systems, so why don't we just concentrate on Grandmother?" Ann said.

"Let's. There's something we haven't thought about," Kate said. "Wouldn't you say that every nightclub has cameras on every floor?"

"Whoa! Go on!" Ann said with excitement in her voice.

"And monitors in a private office upstairs?" Kate said.

"Yes! Yes!" Ann said in a loud voice. "And if the owner or manager would permit our staying upstairs and watching the monitors, a miracle would be born!"

"Wait, my beautiful daughter, there's more."

"I'm waiting with bated breath," Ann said.

"All those nightclubs are owned by just a few people. One man owns several of them. A family owns several more," Kate said.

"I'm still listening," Ann said.

"While we're watching monitors, we're perfectly safe, so why don't we ask if security guards will walk one of us to a second nightclub. That way, we'll be watching two clubs at the same time. After an hour or so, we'll both be escorted to another club."

"Mother, you're a genius!" Ann said in a loud voice.

"Well, you would have thought about it yourself with just a little more time," Kate said.

"No, no, Mother, you get all the credit, but I have another tidbit. Let's park in the middle of Broadway and spread out from there."

"Fine idea. We've just refined our search using only a few minutes," Kate said, "and, honey, getting permission from the managers will be a no-brainer."

"You have all my attention again," Ann said.

"No manager would want the word to get out that someone was abducted in their club. They'll be like little pushovers. When we ask them, they'll say, 'No problem, lady.'"

Ann laughed. "You're a con if ever there was one, Mother. Hey, look! Someone left a parking space just for us."

"And look, honey. We're parking in front of a club that's one of several that's owned by a single corporation," Kate said.

"Well, let's just go pay the manager a visit. We have fifteen minutes before they open," Ann said.

"Let's just sit and observe the people until they open. This is going to work out just great."

Ann parked, talked small talk until the bar opened, and went inside and walked to the bar. A young woman introduced herself as the barkeeper.

"Good morning. We're looking for the manager. Can you tell us where we might find him or her?" Kate said.

"He's a man," the barkeeper said. "He's the one with the white shirt and dark trousers standing at the table with the four guys. Hey! You're the lady that owns the café, aren't you?" the barkeeper said.

Kate smiled. "Thank you for knowing that. I'm Kate, and this is my daughter, Ann."

"No way!" the barkeeper said in a loud voice. "You two could pass for sisters."

"For some reason we hear that a lot," Kate said and smiled.

"I wouldn't have the faintest idea why. Hey! Hold on! I'll walk you over and introduce you to Pete. He's the manager," the barkeeper said. "Hey, my name's Mandy. Drinks are on the house if you're thirsty."

"Thank you so much," Kate said. "We may take you up on your generous hospitality for some tea later."

"Anytime! It'll be our pleasure," Mandy said.

Mandy took them to Pete. "Pete, this is Kate. She owns Sara's café that has the famous tea, and this is her daughter, Ann. They want to talk with you," Mandy said, and then she quickly returned to the bar.

"What can I do for you two ladies?" Pete said.

Kate explained that Sara had gotten separated from them and was missing, but the police were not to be notified under any circumstances. She and Ann could handle anything that might come up. "So, here's a big request," Kate said. "We believe a woman who is an escapee felon may have something to do with Sara's disappearance. Is it possible that we could watch your security monitors for an hour or so to see if we could spot the woman?"

"Of course, you're welcome to watch the monitors," Pete said in an accommodating manner. "I'll call the guy who's in charge of the office and let him know what's going on."

Kate looked at Ann, and both smiled.

"There's another request," Kate said.

"Which is?" Pete said.

"The club across the street is associated with this club. Would you mind if a couple of your security officers accompany one of us to that club so that we can watch two clubs at the same time?"

"I'll get it arranged," Pete said. "Now, you must promise me there'll be no shooting or any other altercation that would get the press involved, and I sure don't want the police snooping around the place."

"You have our word. There'll be no activity on our side to create any disruption of your business or anyone else's business," Kate said.

"Good. Do you want me to arrange for you to watch the monitors of all the clubs we own?" Pete said.

"That would make our whole morning. We couldn't be more thankful," Kate said.

"Consider it done," Pete said. "Now, who's watching here, and who's watching at the club across the street?"

"I'll go across the street, Mother, if that's okay with you," Ann said.

"That's fine, honey," Kate said.

"Shall we text the name and location of the club when we move from the first club?" Ann asked.

"Absolutely. We don't want another person going missing," Kate said.

"If I may interject, ladies, I'll have a security guard stationed right outside the office door, and I'll have two guards accompany you when you move or whenever you leave the office for whatever reason," Pete said.

"You are a dream," Kate said and kissed him on the cheek.

"I'm happy I could help," Pete said and smiled.

For the next five hours, Kate and Ann watched at six different clubs. They met at Ann's car late in the day.

"Are you disappointed, Mother?" Ann asked.

"Of course, I am, honey. You know the clubs are just a long shot. Sally Sue could be in Wyoming for all we know. The next time you see those two sedans, please get their license tag numbers," Kate said.

"Oh, my, my. As experienced as I am in working for the underworld, I didn't think to write the numbers down. I suppose I can chalk it up as not thinking," Ann said.

"Honey, you were caught off guard. For the future, we have to be smart," Kate said.

"I promise," Ann said, and then she drove to Kate's house.

"Let's go to your house, honey. We'll both go in and check everything out, leave all the lights on, and then come back to my house. Will you please spend the night with me?" Kate asked.

"That would be safer. I'll get clothes for tomorrow and for tomorrow night as well," Ann said. She made a U-turn and drove to her house. Both Kate and she went into the house with their weapons drawn. Each weapon had a clip with seventeen rounds; the safety was off; and there was a round in the chamber ready to be fired.

The search of the house yielded nothing.

Ann got her clothes, and they drove back to Kate's house where they did the same search as they had done at Ann's house. Everything was in order.

"Let's brush our teeth and jump in bed," Kate said.

"I'll sleep on the couch because it's nearest your room. That okay?" Ann said.

"And I'll leave my door standing open. If either of us hears a noise, we'll come to each other's rescue," Kate said.

"That'll work," Ann said. "I'll use the guest bathroom to brush my teeth and tidy up."

Each of them got ready for bed and turned in with the hopes of getting at least five hours of sleep. They bade each other goodnight practically yelling from their respective rooms.

At five o'clock, a vehicle horn awakened them.

In her pajamas, Kate met Ann, who had gotten up off the couch.

"Whatta you think?" Ann asked.

"I think we better look around," Kate said. "I'll turn the yard lights on. Do you mind standing on the porch with your revolver while I look around?" Kate asked.

"Of course, I will. Let's go," Ann said.

Kate walked out of the house and into the front yard. In addition to the outside lights, Kate brought a very bright flashlight. She walked around the yard and then went down a small dip that bordered the sidewalk. She bent over and picked up something and hurried back to Ann.

"Honey, do you know what this is?" Kate asked, her words barely audible and slipping out in slow motion. She held up a piece of material for Ann to see.

"Grandmother's blouse! It's Grandmother's blouse you're holding! Why? How?" Ann said loudly.

"Look, honey. There are two bloodstains on it," Kate said, her words still barely audible.

"Okay, Mother, we're at war. Let's ask the chief to see if his lab can lift fingerprints off of it and tell us who they belong to," Ann said.

Kate and Ann met with Chief Martin, who agreed to help.

The fingerprint report came back in two days. There were three different prints on the blouse: Sara's, Sally Sue's, and those of an unidentified person.

"Our work has been cut out for us," Kate said. "While we were snooping around downtown like amateurs, Sally Sue took the offensive and stole Mother away from right under our noses."

"Well, let's review what we know," Ann said. "First, Grandmother was on the north side of Broadway. Second, we arrived in the dark and stuck out like sore thumbs. Sally Sue was watching us when we split up. Grandmother was a sitting duck. She was alone and couldn't see who was lurking in an alley or even know who was behind her. The sidewalk was full of people. The whole scene just made for a bad outcome."

"Well, we changed our technique by watching monitors rather than parading down a sidewalk. Let's make another change. Rather than arrive in the morning, let's start our observation at four in the afternoon," Kate said.

"Good idea. Sally Sue is not going to vanish just because she knows we're looking for her. She has a business which provides her with a livelihood, so that is to our advantage," Ann said.

"And every minute is urgent," Kate said. "Is Mother being tortured? Is she being fed? Is she being given something to drink? If we concentrate on those thoughts, we'll go crazy and never find her."

"So, let's discard all those thoughts and concentrate on apprehending Sally Sue," Ann said.

"Let's do just that. There's something else. Sally Sue knows your vehicle and license tag number, so let's rent a car and at least try to throw her off," Kate said.

"Good idea! Mother, do you think we should have another vote on Sally Sue?"

"Yes, I do. I'll go first," Kate said.

After Kate and Ann voted, Kate announced the results. Two black marbles had been voted which meant that Sally Sue would perish after her apprehension.

Since they had several hours before going to Broadway, they visited Sara's house and toured it. They didn't notice anything unusual. After that, they visited Ann's house. It too appeared to be okay.

"Mother, what we didn't consider is cameras inside the house. Everything could look perfect, and we haven't any idea we're being filmed," Ann said.

"You're right, and we have to be careful in our conversation in the event there are listening devices. Once we apprehend Sally Sue and the person driving the car that was spying on us, we won't have any worries," Kate said.

"We have to decide what we're going to do with the driver once the person is captured," Ann said.

"I have an idea," Kate said.

"I have one too," Ann said.

"So, once we apprehend Sally Sue and the driver, we'll see what each of us thought about what to do with the driver," Kate said.

"Yes, we will. It's two o'clock. Shouldn't we be on our way to get the rental car?" Ann said.

"Yes, we should. I'm ready," Kate said.

They drove to a rental dealer and rented a make of a vehicle that was common on the street. The windows on this vehicle were also heavily tinted.

"This should throw her off just a little, and our new daylight hours should help also," Kate said.

"I think both changes will help us, and I'm hoping tonight is the night we see Sally Sue," Ann said.

It was two-thirty in the morning when Kate and Ann arrived back at Kate's house. They had watched monitors throughout the night and had no hits.

"I'm glad I left the outside lights on. They are sort of a welcome sign getting home this late at night," Kate said.

"Mother, what is that white object in your yard?" Ann asked.

"Stop! Stop here! I'll walk across the grass and get it," Kate said, her voice unusually loud and demanding.

Ann stopped the car, and Kate hurried out of the car, across the lawn, and returned holding a white object.

"It's Mother's bra," Kate said. "I know her brand."

Ann pounded the steering wheel with the palms of her hands. "No! No! How can it be? How can it be? How can she continue to be ahead of us?" Ann said, her voice sounding frustrated. "I got it! I got it!" Ann said loudly. "We have a mole somewhere on Broadway!"

"A mole? Well now, you may be on to something. Tomorrow, let me out on lower Broadway, give me ten minutes to walk up the north side of Broadway, and try to park as close as possible to the place we parked yesterday," Kate said.

"It's a plan," Ann said.

The next afternoon, Ann drove to lower Broadway, and Kate got out of the car. "Keep in touch," Ann said.

Kate held a thumbs-up signal to acknowledge that she would, and then she began walking up Broadway.

Ann drove up Broadway, made a U-turn at Eighth Avenue and parked between Third and Fifth Avenue. She had previously worked the clubs on the south side of Broadway, and she decided to work the club near where she parked. Before she got to the entrance door, her phone rang.

"I found the mole," Kate said in a low tone of voice.

"You did!" Ann said in a loud voice.

"I did. He has a travel agency kiosk. He had his phone focused on you, and as soon as you got out of the car, he started taking pictures."

"What are you doing now?" Ann asked.

"We'll talk later. I confronted him, took his phone and threw it down the drain sewer, but we'll talk later," Kate said.

"Tell me when we meet," Ann said.

"Meet me on this side of the street on the corner when you get to Fifth Avenue," Kate said.

"On my way," Ann said.

A few moments passed, and Ann crossed the street and met Kate who motioned for her to follow. They walked north on Fifth Avenue until Kate made a right turn into a parking lot. She motioned Ann to follow her to the backside of a building that had no windows or doors.

"Get in front of me, honey, so no one can see my mouth talking," Kate said.

Ann moved to within a foot of her mother's face and then looked around to see if they could be overheard or if anyone could see their mouths as they talked. She looked at the roof above them and then checked out the buildings on the opposite side of the street. There wasn't anything unusual.

"I can't believe it. The mole was right across from where we parked," Kate said.

"What're we going to do?" Ann asked.

Kate looked from one side to the opposite side of where they stood and then focused her attention on the parking lot. Satisfied they were not being observed, she said, "Snuff him." Her voice was low and deliberate.

Ann looked around and then looked back at her mother. "How?" she asked.

Kate repeated her surveillance of their position, and then she said, "Get him into the street so he'll get eliminated by a very large vehicle."

"How do we get him to go into the street with moving traffic?" Ann said in a whisper.

"That's a good question," Kate said.

"What if I get on one side of the street, and you get on the other side? He'll be with you on your side with you urging him into the street. I'll be on my side urging him to come to me, but we have to make sure there's a big enough vehicle to do him in."

"Honey, that won't work. Someone on the sidewalk will notice what we're doing, and the jig will be up."

Ann looked at Kate for a moment and said, "Of course, you're right. We'd be noticed right off the bat. Looks like I need to put out our flags for a better idea. But a lesser problem is: when does he get off work? We just can't take care of him while everyone is standing on the sidewalk gawking."

"You just knew my thought, didn't you?" Kate said.

Ann smiled. "I have a thought. He has to know who I am from taking pictures every time I get outta my car. But you on the other hand are probably an intimidator to him. Whatta you think?"

Kate hesitated for a moment and said, "You're probably right. What do you have up your sleeve?"

"Whatta you think about you going to the kiosk and asking him about a trip or cruise you're considering? Once you get his attention, simply ask him what time he gets off work. Tell him you want to talk it over with a friend, and you'll be back to talk with him."

"You're one little devious daughter. Have I told you that in days gone by?"

"No, you haven't, but my interpretation of that is that it's not good. I always thought I was as straightforward as they come, but I am my mother's daughter," Ann said, and then she giggled.

Kate smiled. "You're special, you know. Say, what you suggested might work. He thinks I threw his phone away simply because he was being nosy. I promised him a new phone. So, for the mole, I'm doing exactly as you suggested. Why don't you work a coupla clubs while I get our much-needed information, and then I'll meet you in one hour on the north side of Broadway and on the east side of Fourth Avenue.

We cannot rely on text messaging anymore. Too much evidence in those little electronic gadgets."

"You're exactly right. If we ever got in a jam, our phones would tattle on us. Before this is over, your phone will show that you will have been at the mole's place three or four times. That would be a perfect clue for the police," Ann said.

"You are so correct. When we finish this assignment, we need to dispose of the phones. We could take a four-pound sledgehammer and crush it beyond recognition and then bury it or take it to a bridge over the Cumberland River and drop it squarely in the middle. Either way, we need to beat every little piece of the inside of the phone to a pulp," Kate said.

"And if it's plastic, beat it to shreds," Ann said.

"Can the phone company detect from the phone signals that it's being destroyed?" Kate asked.

"I don't know, but that's something we definitely need to find out," Ann said.

"Definitely," Kate said.

"Okay, I'll cross over," Ann said. "Just text my name so that I'll know to meet you…straight across from here on the sidewalk. This is going to be a one-horse show, you know, because he knows me, and if I show up with you, he'll know something's up."

"I've thought about that already. I have to be careful about someone seeing me talk with him on the sidewalk and then him running into the street," Kate said.

"Well, Mother Nature has to be on your side. We have to wait until dark. No one's going to focus on you talking to the mole as they walk by. And, as soon as the mole steps into the street, you take off like a jet from an aircraft carrier," Ann said.

"You make it sound so easy, my daughter."

"We're gifted in what we do. Grandmother said that. You said that. We're gifted. This will go over just like clockwork," Ann said.

"Okay, let's get with it," Kate said. "I'll see you in a few."

Ann crossed the street and went into a nightclub that had given her the freedom to use an administrative office with cameras that provided surveillance of the patrons in every part of the nightclub. She surveyed the areas where patrons milled around, but she did not notice any person that might fit the description of Sally Sue. About thirty minutes later, her phone texted her name. She immediately took the elevator to the first floor, went outside, and met Kate.

"Follow me," Kate said.

Ann followed Kate to a bench that sat in a nook off the sidewalk and away from the flow of sidewalk traffic.

Kate sat down and motioned Ann to sit, which she did.

"What's up?" Ann asked.

"He told me he has to go home to check on his laundry. He'll be back in one hour," Kate said.

"Well, Sally Sue already knows we're in town, thanks to the mole. If she's really here, do you think she stays in town when she knows we're here?" Ann said.

"I think she's too brazen to turn tail and run. I have a hunch that she's very confident after all these years of evading justice. As for us, she's not the least bit concerned about us because she has the mole, and she knows where we are. She probably snickers at the very thought of us being in town without a clue as to her whereabouts."

"Now, that gets my pressure up," Ann said. "She probably knows every step we take, and we haven't the foggiest idea where to even look for her."

"It's the nature of the game we play," Kate said. "Say, I have thirty more minutes before I meet him. I'll hang around here for fifteen minutes and then go back across the street."

"Do you have a plan?" Ann asked.

"I've had several," Kate said. "I believe I've settled on one and in a very short period of time, I'll know if I picked the right one."

"You'll let me know?" Ann said.

"Of course. Okay, I'm headed back. I'll keep in touch," Kate said, and then she crossed the street and went back to the travel agency kiosk.

"Hey, there you are," a voice said.

"Oh, I'm so sorry. I should have been here waiting for you. Can we talk here in the cool air of the night?" Kate asked.

"Oh, sure, sure, no problem. Do you need some more information, or have you made up your mind?" the man asked.

"Oh, I think we're ready, that is, my husband and I. We both like the Alaskan cruise…the fourteen-day one, so I think we're ready to do whatever we have to do. He would like to meet you though, and I have a great surprise for you! I have more business for you!"

"Oh, terrific. How so?"

"My family is having a family reunion in two months, and I believe they would all enjoy a cruise…just one week, though."

"A week is fine. How many people are in the family?" the man asked.

"Twenty-eight," Kate said.

"Twenty-eight! Wow! I would be most happy to accommodate them," the man said.

"I also would like to hook up with a very dear friend of mine. She may want to go too. Her name's Sally Sue Bottoms, and I haven't the faintest idea where to find her."

"Oh, I can help you. She works out of that nightclub right across from us."

"Really. Does she work any other clubs?" Kate asked.

"No, no. Just that one," the man said.

"Thank you so much. You just don't know how much I appreciate the information. Thank you. Thank you," Kate said.

"My pleasure," the man said.

"Okay, shall we get the Alaskan cruise settled?" Kate said.

"Yes, yes. Your husband? Where is he?" the man asked.

"He's across the street. Do you mind going across and talking with him?" Kate asked, and as she talked, she was counting the seconds it took for a speeding vehicle to reach their location from a block and a half away. She also counted the seconds it took when vehicles had to stop for a stop light and then accelerate from a dead stop.

"He can't come over here?" the man asked.

"No, no, he has a very bad hip, and it hurts when he walks," Kate said, and then she squeezed the muscle in her cheek to cause her to appear seriously concerned about her husband. "I will watch for the traffic for you," she said.

"I will go to the light and cross over," the man said.

"No, no, just cross here. My husband's in pain, and he's waiting for you to come over."

"Okay, I'll go," the man said.

"Great! Back up to the curb, and I'll tell you when it's safe to go, and when I tell you, go like you're shot out of a cannon," Kate said.

"I can go on my own," the man said.

"No, no, the lights will blind you, and you won't know if you're coming or going," Kate said. "Trust me. I'll get you over safely."

"Okay, I'll do it your way," the man said.

Kate looked around her to see if pedestrians were near, and she was satisfied that there was no one near that would notice her and the man talking. She then looked up Broadway and saw a tour bus coming in their direction. By her previous observation, the bus would be at their location in four seconds after it cleared the green traffic light above from where they stood. She waited until the bus was underneath the green traffic light, and then she said, "It's safe to go. Go! Go!"

The man turned and ran into the street. Once he was in the path of the bus, it was obvious he recognized he was in danger. He hesitated and started to run back and then hesitated again and changed his direction in an attempt to run to the opposite side of the street. The bus hit the man, who no doubt was blinded by the lights, squarely in the torso. The tremendous force knocked him to the pavement, and he then was run over by the bus and by a vehicle that was being pulled in tandem with the bus. It was immaterial whether the bus driver saw the man because he could not brake fast enough to avoid hitting the man.

As soon as the man stepped off the curb, Kate walked quickly up the street to the traffic light and crossed to the opposite side of the street. She hurried to meet Ann.

Ann put her mouth close to Kate's ear and said, "The mole's gone."

"I know, and do I have some wonderful news for you," Kate said.

"Well?"

"Ms. Sally Sue Cross Bottoms works right out of the club behind us. That is her headquarters, and she works no other clubs. Whatta you think about that?" Kate said.

Ann laughed and reached out for her mother's hand. "You're a genius! You're a number one genius! How did you find that out?"

"The mole."

Ann laughed again. "You twisted his arm?"

"No, I just asked him, and he told me," Kate said.

"Fantastic! Whatta we do now?" Ann asked.

"Well, we don't know the impact of the mole's accident as far as Sally Sue is concerned. If I were her, I'd skip town because the odds have just increased with her being on her own. Of course, she may have more than one mole. We'll find that out, I'm sure."

"Shall we go upstairs and just watch until midnight?" Ann asked.

"Let's. We have to find Mother. We don't have any idea what her condition is. We don't know if she is tied up somewhere; we don't know if she's being fed; we don't know anything," Kate said.

They went to the club's administrative office and watched the monitors until midnight and then went home.

CHAPTER 14

For the next two nights after the mole's demise in the middle of Broadway, Kate and Ann watched monitors until two-thirty in the morning.

"Honey, I know you're getting frustrated, but we can't allow ourselves to give up on this effort to find Mother. We must find her soon, though, because the odds are beginning to sway to the opposite side and not in our favor," Kate said as they drove home on the second night.

"Oh, I'm just tired, Mother. I will never give up on our quest to find Grandmother. I do suggest we use the pulley this time," Ann said.

"Oh, no doubt. We must treat this Sally Sue the same as she treated her two little children that she drowned. She must go feet first in a lake or river and realize that soon she will no longer be around," Kate said.

"The problem is finding a place," Ann said. "We already know the riverfront off First Avenue is excessively traveled, and the terrain is so bad going north of there that it won't permit us to drag a third person along."

"We could go to the river at Route 109, but it is so populated where we're able to use it," Kate said.

"I just got an idea!" Ann said, her voice loud and filled with excitement.

"What's that?" Kate asked.

"There's a walking trail that's not used a lot just across the road from the state park off Murfreesboro Road, and there's a wonderful cliff that drops off in the water that looks to be very deep. There are trees nearby, also. We could drive there just at dusk, walk to the cliff, and introduce Sally Sue to the area. I haven't seen any boats on the lake at night, so that should not be an issue."

The next afternoon, Kate climbed into Ann's car, looked at her daughter, and said, "Let's get 'er tonight."

"Well, good afternoon, Mother," Ann said as she put the car in gear and started driving. "Wait a second," she said, pulling over to the curb. "I'm going to call Molly and ask her to pick up Cynthia and both of them stay at my house until we get back. I'd feel better if someone was with them, but we have to do what we have to do."

"Good idea," Kate said. "I meant what I said. We've been at this too long. It's time to find Sally Sue; it's time to find Mother; it's time to resume our lives."

"I agree one hundred percent, but we're doing all we know to do, Mother. Before we found Sally Sue's point of operations, we were just floundering up and down Broadway. Now at least we have something concrete to hang our hats on," Ann said.

"Honey, we don't have hats. Even if we did, we wouldn't hang them on concrete."

Even as she maneuvered through heavy traffic, Ann looked at her mother and then looked back at the street. "Mother, I share your frustration, but we can't get down. It's only a matter of time before we look down at the people inside the bar and say, 'There she is. There's Sally Sue.'"

Kate looked at Ann, showed no expression for a few moments, and then smiled. "That'll be the day, won't it? Yes, that'll be the day...well, in this case, the night."

"Yeah, it sure will be the night," Ann said.

They completed the trip into the city, parked, and went inside the club that Sally Sue used for her main base of operations. They hurried upstairs, because if Sally Sue were hanging around, she would notice them right away.

"Do you want the first floor or the second floor?" Kate said as she pointed to monitors that displayed activity on the different floors of the club.

"I'll take the second floor," Ann said. "You've predicted that this is the night, and I'll wager Sally Sue's going to be hanging around the bar on the first floor. When you see her, you'll say, 'I told you so.'"

Kate smiled. "You scoff at my prediction. Just wait. You'll see," she said.

They watched monitors until eight o'clock, at which time the barkeeper sent up a tuna sandwich, chips, and tea for each of them. They continued to watch as they ate. When one person needed a break, the second person would watch monitors that surveyed both floors.

At ten o'clock, Ann said, "Mother, the night's not over yet."

"I'm still saying this is the night, honey. Just keep on watching that monitor. You never know what you'll see."

Midnight came, and they alternated taking breaks. When Ann returned from her break, Kate said, "The traffic's picking up. Do people ever sleep around here?"

"Some of these people just have one big party after another, it seems," Ann said.

The time dragged on until it was finally one-thirty.

"Honey, I'm beginning to wear down. Do you want to call it a night?" Kate said.

"Let's just stay another fifteen or twenty minutes. Can you make it that long?" Ann said.

"I'll try," Kate said, and then she leaned back and yawned. As she moved back to watch, she grabbed both sides of the monitor.

"What? What is it, Mother?" Ann said, her voice sounding concerned.

"Look! Look! The lady at the bar with the short skirt! Her hand! Look at her hand! It's Sally Sue! Let's go! Go! Put your suppressor on your gun as we go," Kate said, her breath coming fast.

They ran to the elevator, revolver in one hand, and a suppressor in the other hand.

"Let's go, elevator. Go! Go!" Kate said, jumping up and down. "Honey, you get on one side of her, and I'll get on the other!" she said, her voice nearly gasping for breath, and then she beat on the elevator door. "Open, open!" she yelled.

Before she could finish her words, the elevator door opened. She jumped backwards, and her face appeared as if in shock.

Ann grabbed her mother by the shoulder. "Let's go, Mother! Let's go!"

They rushed into the elevator and stood a moment before Ann pushed the "close door" repeatedly. Kate stomped the floor.

"Mother, get your suppressor on!" Ann said in a hurried voice. "Hurry! Hurry!" she said. She stuck her revolver in the suppressor-compatible holster she had strapped over her shoulder and then covered it with her jacket.

Just as the elevator stopped on the first floor, Kate put the revolver in her holster and pulled her jacket over it. She looked at Ann only for an instant and then motioned for her to follow. "Sally Sue better still be there," she whispered.

They wound their way through the crowd until they were close to the bar and then suddenly, they were in an opening and could see Sally Sue, who faced the bar and had her back turned to them.

"Hide your gun with your purse," Kate said in a low tone of voice.

Kate motioned for Ann to go to the right of Sally Sue, and instantly they were standing on either side of her with their revolvers drawn, and then each stuck the barrel of their revolver into her side.

"You're going with us, Sally Sue," Kate said in a low but firm voice.

Sally Sue didn't move for a moment, but then she turned practically in slow motion, moved the slim purse that was held at her waist with a shoulder strap, and looked at Kate.

Kate and Ann moved their revolvers as Sally Sue moved and now the barrels were against her midsection and spine.

Sally Sue, appearing calm and confident, looked at Kate for another instant and then spit in her face.

Seeing it, Ann moved to the side of Sally Sue and said, "Shoot her!"

Suddenly, a man with a nine-millimeter strapped to his waist appeared. "Is there a problem here?" he asked in a husky voice.

"No, there's no problem. Who are you?" Kate asked.

"I'm security, ma'am. Do you need help here?"

"We need for this lady to go outside with us," Ann said hurriedly.

The security man motioned with his hand, and another man with a nine-millimeter joined them. "These are Pete's friends," he said, pointing to Kate and Ann.

"These ladies need for this lady to join them outside," he told the other man and motioned to Sally Sue.

"You got it," the second man said, and then he and the first man put their arms under Sally Sue's armpit and carried her outside. Kate and Ann followed.

Once outside, the first security man said, "Where do you want her, ma'am?"

"Over next to that car," Kate said, pointing to Ann's car.

The men again hoisted Sally Sue off her feet and carried her to the curb where Ann's car was parked. Miraculously, the sidewalk was barren of pedestrians.

"We'll take it from here," Ann said as she opened the rear door of her car.

"Let us know if you need anything else," the first security man said.

"Thank you," Kate said. "You don't know how much we appreciate what you've done."

Both men turned and walked away.

Immediately, Ann grabbed the back of Sally Sue's head and shoved it viciously into the top of the car above the door opening. As she did, Kate ran to the opposite side of the car and opened the door.

"Ohhh!" Sally Sue grunted loudly.

"I'm so sorry. Did that hurt?" Ann said.

Holding Sally Sue by the back of her hair, she again slammed her face into the top of the car.

"Ohhh! Ohhh!" Sally Sue continued to grunt loudly.

As Ann was punishing Sally Sue, Kate climbed into the back seat of the car, across the seat, and yelled loudly at Ann, "Give me her left arm!"

Ann twisted Sally Sue so that she faced the rear of the car and then lifted Sally Sue's left arm so that Kate could grasp it.

"Now, shut the door against her arm!" Kate yelled.

Ann pulled Sally Sue by the hair until only her arm was inside the car, and then she slammed the door catching the arm close to her bicep.

"Ohhh! Ohhh! Ohhh!" Sally Sue yelled.

"Again!" Kate yelled.

Ann pulled the door open and then slammed it as hard as she could.

Sally Sue drooped and was about to sink to the ground. Seeing her, Ann grabbed her around the waist and scooted her in the back seat. "Stay with her. We're outta here," Ann said loudly to her mother.

Kate immediately straightened herself in the back seat, shut the door, and Ann just as rapidly started the car and pulled into the lane going east down to First Avenue going out of the city.

"Where's my mother?" Kate asked in a firm voice, her teeth clenched.

Sally Sue, now barely conscious, turned slowly to look at Kate but said nothing.

"I'll ask you a second time. Where's my mother?" Kate said.

Still, there was no response from Sally Sue.

"That's fine. You'll get a second dose when we get home," Kate said, and then she told Ann to drive to Kate's house.

Ann watched her speed to avoid getting stopped and having to explain a semi-conscious woman in the back seat. Twenty-five minutes later, she guided the car into Kate's driveway. She threw open her door and then jerked the back door open where Sally Sue was hunched over. As if in unison, Kate opened her door.

"You're in a private place, Sally Sue. You're going to tell us where mother is or we're going to break every bone in your body," Kate said.

Sally Sue remained hunched over and didn't move.

"Pull 'er out. We're going to work on her arm some more," Kate told Ann.

Ann grabbed Sally Sue's hair and began to tug.

"Uh…uh…car. In my…car," Sally Sue uttered, her words barely audible.

"You said your car? Where's your car?" Kate said in a demanding voice.

Sally Sue didn't move, nor did she try to talk.

Again, Ann jerked her hair and began pulling her out of the back seat.

"Behin'…behin' th'…th' club," Sally Sue uttered. "Whi…car."

"White car?" Kate said.

"Yea…" Sally Sue said.

"I'm calling Molly to come over here with Cynthia immediately," Ann said.

They went into the house.

"Let's tie Sally Sue to the bedrail. Tell Molly to wash the blood off this lady's face when she gets here," Kate said.

"Sally Sue, where are the keys to your car?" Kate said, again using her demanding voice.

"Uh…uh, arm, my arm…hurts…ohhh…ohhh."

"We're going to give you something for the arm, Sally Sue. Where're the keys to your car?" Kate said.

Ann put her hand on Sally Sue's head and applied pressure.

"Pur...purs..."

"Honey, look in her purse," Kate said, looking at Ann.

Instead of putting the shoulder strap of her purse over her shoulder, Sally Sue had put the strap over her head, so no one could have grabbed her purse without pulling her head off. Throughout the punishment by Ann, the purse remained intact on her.

Ann unzipped the purse and poured the contents on the floor. "Ahh, keys and a fob to open the doors," Ann said. "I hear someone coming. That must be Molly," she said, and then she walked hurriedly to the front door. Before Molly could ring the doorbell, Ann opened the door.

"We got here as fast as we could straight from your house," Molly said.

"She flew," Cynthia said.

"That's good. That's great. Look, we have a person who has injured herself, and she's also a bad person. Her name's Sally Sue. We want both of you to watch her while we go into town. Will you do that for us?" Ann said.

"Of course," Molly said.

"Yes, ma'am," Cynthia said.

"Molly, she has some blood on her forehead and face. Do you mind using hydrogen peroxide to clean her up? It's underneath the sink in the bathroom," Ann said.

"Yes, ma'am. I can do that."

"Do not touch her blood. While you're cleaning, make sure you don't touch her blood with your hands. There's a box of gloves under the kitchen sink. Get a trash bag outta the kitchen and put your cleaning materials in the bag."

"Okay. No problem," Molly said.

"Because she's a bad person, she's tied to the rail in the bedroom. Cynthia, if she has to go to the bathroom, untie her but stay with her every minute. Go inside the bathroom with her. If she starts to run, grab her and tie her up again."

"Stay with her and go to the bathroom with her. I can do that," Cynthia said.

"Great! Both of you are a great help. Thank you," Ann said, and then she yelled to Kate. "We're ready, Mother. Let's go."

Kate came hurriedly from the bedroom, and she and Ann left the house, got in the car, and drove to town.

"There's an alley right beside the club. We will probably drive through it to get to the back of the club. Do you agree?" Ann said.

"Yes. I would say that's the only way to get to it," Kate said.

"This place is unreal," Ann said. "It's nearly three o'clock in the morning, and the street is full of traffic. Can you believe it, Mother?"

"It is unreal. I do hope we find Mother unharmed," Kate said.

Ann maneuvered her car through the traffic and drove into the alley beside the club. "Here we go," she said.

"Okay, we're looking for a white car," Kate said.

"Mother, just press the button on the fob, and the lights will come on."

"Of course. How dumb can one be?"

Once they traversed the alley, a space opened up which served as a parking area for employees and special patrons. There were twenty to twenty-five parking spaces available, but there were only three cars parked, and none of them was white. Kate pressed the fob repeatedly, but nothing happened.

"She has led us on a wild goose chase," Kate said. "Let's go back home. I'm gonna work on Ms. Sally Sue."

Ann drove them back to Kate's house, and Kate stormed out of the car, up the steps, and into her house. Stopping for a moment, she reminded herself that Molly and Cynthia were in the house, and she should drill down her anger and appear calm in front of them. She continued walking to the bedroom with Ann, who had caught up with her.

"How's the patient?" Kate asked.

"I cleaned her and gave her two Tylenol," Molly said. "She's better, but she has a very sore arm. I believe it may be broken."

"We'll get an arm brace and wrap it good," Kate said. "Do you mind excusing us a minute? I need to talk with Sally Sue."

Molly and Cynthia looked puzzled.

"You want us to leave?" Molly asked.

"If you don't mind," Kate said.

"Okay, we're gone. Let's go, Cynthia," Molly said.

After Molly and Cynthia were out of earshot, Kate turned to Sally Sue and said, "Your car's not behind the club, Sally Sue. Now, if you don't come clean with us, we're going to do serious damage to your body. Do you understand me? Trust me. You don't want Ann to get hold of you. So, let's go over this one more time. My mother is in your car? Is that right?"

"Ye…yeh…" Sally Sue uttered.

"And where's your car?"

"Buu…"

"I can't hear you. Where's your car?"

"Bub…Bubba…"

"Bubba? Bubba has your car?"

"Yeh."

"Where did Bubba take your car?" Kate asked.

"Mt. Jul…Mt. Julet Fir…Fire Department."

"Mt. Juliet Fire Department? Bubba has your car at Mt. Juliet Fire Department?"

"Yeh."

"He's on duty there?"

"Yeh."

"And Mother's in the car?"

"Yeh."

"He better be there Sally Sue, and Mother better be there. If I come back a second time, it's not going to be pretty for you. Do you understand? So, if you've not been straight with me, you're gonna be in more pain that you can't imagine."

"Okaa…" Sally Sue said.

Kate walked out of the bedroom and met Ann, Molly, and Cynthia. "Honey, we're off again," she told Ann. "Can you ladies pick up where you left off?" she said, looking at Molly and Cynthia.

"Yes, ma'am," Molly said, her voice sounding confident and cheerful.

"Yes, ma'am," Cynthia said.

"Let's go, honey," Kate said.

They left the house and got into Ann's car.

"Where to?" Ann asked.

"Supposedly, Mother's in Sally Sue's car, and Bubba has the car at Mt. Juliet Fire Department.

Ann drove to Mt. Juliet Fire Department. As she drove up, a fire truck came rolling out of the garage, its siren wailing loudly and ominously in the once peaceful night.

"Hey, that might be good for us. If Bubba's on the truck, that'll be great because Bubba won't be here to harass us when we're looking around Sally Sue's car."

"Honey, don't you remember my telling you that we have a special spirit, and things fall our way?"

"You did…at least something close to that," Ann said.

"Okay, there are cars parked in the rear. Let's check them out," Kate said.

Ann drove to the area where cars were parked, and Kate immediately pressed the fob to Sally Sue's car. Suddenly, lights lit up on a car that was parked between two other cars.

"Mother! Look! That's it! That's the car!" Ann said, her voice full of excitement.

"Stop the car, honey! Let's get Mother!" Kate said, her voice loud and anxious.

Ann stopped the car, and they both jumped out. Ann ran to the driver's side, and Kate ran to the passenger said of the lighted car. They looked in the cab and then the backseat and floorboard of the car. Sara was not there.

"She's pulled our chain again," Kate said.

"Let's go home, Mother. I have a device that'll make her talk or else," Ann said.

Kate looked at Ann and shook her head from one side to the other to show her disgust.

They began walking back to the car, but Kate stopped suddenly. "We didn't check the trunk," Kate said.

"Surely not," Ann said, her voice full of disbelief. "Surely she wouldn't put Grandmother in the trunk."

Kate used the fob to open the trunk, and they walked back to Sally Sue's car.

"Wha…Mother?" Kate uttered, and then she whirled around immediately and said, "Honey, it's Mother! Oh, my word! She's just lying there all crumpled up."

A motion light on the back of the building flickered and then shined brightly, allowing Kate to look inside the trunk.

"Mother, is she…is she…" Ann muttered, emotionally unable to complete her sentence.

Kate touched her mother. "She's warm. She's still warm," Kate said. "Honey, bring your car up here so that your back seat is aligned with this trunk."

Ann ran to her car and drove to the back of Sally Sue's car, aligned her back seat to the open trunk where Sara lay, then stopped. She jumped out and ran to stand beside Kate, who had taken off her blouse and covered her mother.

"Honey, take off your blouse and cover Mother. Please," Kate said.

Ann did as her mother had asked.

"Open your back door, please," Kate said.

Ann immediately opened the door.

"Let's lift her out carefully and get her in the back seat," Kate said.

Ann moved to hold her grandmother's legs while Kate carefully worked her hands inch by inch under Sara's shoulders.

"You ready to lift, honey?"

"I'm ready, Mother."

"Let's go."

Kate gradually lifted her mother's shoulders as Ann lifted Sara's legs and tucked them under her right armpit. She then slowly scooted her hands under her grandmother's hips.

"Let's go, Mother," Ann said.

Very slowly, they lifted Sara up and away from the trunk until they cleared the lip of the opening.

"Okay, let's very slowly get her in the back seat," Kate said.

Moving slowly and carefully, they lifted Sara until her body touched the seat of Ann's car, and then Kate squatted and lifted her mother's shoulders onto the seat.

"Stay where you are. I'm going to the other side to scoot her in," Kate instructed.

"Okay," Ann said as she strained to hold her grandmother's lower body and legs.

Kate ran to the opposite side of the car, opened the door, and climbed onto the seat to reach Sara. "Okay, I'm going to scoot her this way. Please hold her legs."

They eased her further onto the seat but left just enough space for Kate to sit beside her.

"Let's take her to her own house, but drive slowly and carefully, honey," Kate said.

Ann shut the back door and said, "Ready, Mother?"

"Please, let's go," Kate said.

Ann started the car, turned her vehicle, and pulled onto Mt. Juliet Road. As they began to drive away, the fire truck that had left earlier passed them on its return trip to the garage.

"I told you we are protected by a special spirit," Kate said almost in a whisper.

"I believe you, Mother. Should we get Cynthia to help us carry Grandmother into the house?"

"No, honey. We can't get Molly or Cynthia involved. It's up to us."

"We need some medical assistance, don't you think?" Ann said.

"What about Doctor Phillips? Do you think he would come to Mother's house?" Kate asked.

There was silence for several moments, and then Ann said, "Do you think he would even talk to me, Mother?"

"Of course, he would. You explained the problem between you and him. Now, I know you didn't go into great detail, but I feel strongly he's your friend. Just think about it."

There was another long silence. Finally, Ann said, "Okay, Mother, let's get Grandmother in the bed, and I'll go do my best. We have to hurry though. It's getting to be daylight, and he'll be leaving the hospital if we don't hurry."

It only took twenty minutes for Ann to drive to Sara's house where she parked as close to the front door as possible. Looking in the back seat, she said, "Mother, I have an idea. The chairs in the dining room have rollers on them…"

"Oh, my gosh, honey! That's too dangerous. What if we let the chair get away from us, and it rolled down into the street? Or what if she fell outta the chair?"

"Well, Mother, think about it. We have a long walk trying to carry her to her bed. We could very well drop her on the way."

Kate was silent for a moment, and then she said, "Okay, let's do it. We could put her in the chair, wrap a cloth around her and the chair so she couldn't fall out, and then get her to her bed. Now that I think about it, it's a wonderful idea. Will you please bring a chair and a bed sheet?"

"I'll be back in a flash," Ann said.

She disappeared but returned in a few moments pushing a chair with a towel and a white sheet folded and lying on the seat.

"If we can get the towel under her, we can pull her with it," Ann said.

"Another wonderful idea. Now, how are we going to do this? If we pull her out feet first, I'm afraid we'll hurt her legs," Kate said.

"Mother, you ease her out by the shoulders. I'll hold the chair as close to the car as possible. Wait! Wait! I'll be right back," Ann said, and then she rushed into the house. Only a few moments passed, and she returned with two triangular pieces of wood. "These will keep the chair from sliding," she said.

"Great! Get in place, and let's do it," Kate said.

"I'm ready," Ann said.

Kate worked her hands underneath Sara's armpits and began sliding her out of the back seat and toward the chair.

"Mother, can you lift her shoulders, and I'll scoot the towel under her," Ann said.

"Here we go," Kate said.

"Okay, okay, that's great. I got it all the way to her underwear."

"Good. Let me try to pull her into the chair. Please hold the chair," Kate said.

Holding the ends of the towel, Kate slowly and carefully pulled Sara onto the chair. "Okay, let me get her legs, and then you very, very slowly pull the chair away from the car."

Kate held Sara's legs as Ann slowly moved the chair backwards.

"Now, wrap the sheet around her," Kate said.

Ann wrapped the sheet around Sara and the chair and tied it.

"There, we're ready. Let's get her into bed. I'll help with the chair," Kate said.

They pushed Sara to the bedroom which was off to the left of the living room. Ann carefully took off the sheet, and then she pulled the covers back on the bed.

"Can you hold her by the back and leg, and I'll get the other side?" Kate said.

"Let's go," Ann said.

They lifted Sara and put her in the bed, and then Kate covered her with a sheet and comforter.

"Honey, get two of her blouses for us, and then will you go as fast as possible and get Doctor Phillips? I'll be washing Mother," Kate said.

Ann slipped on a blouse, left the house, and drove at a fast clip to the hospital. She parked at the lower end of the Emergency Room parking area and rushed inside. "Be there. Be there," she said almost in a whisper.

Suddenly, Doctor Phillips appeared in street clothes and no white hospital coat.

"Doctor….Doctor Phillips," Ann said loudly.

Doctor Phillips, seeming preoccupied, turned and looked at Ann. His head tilted backwards as if surprised. "Ann? Ann, what are you doing here?"

"I'm sorry. I'm sorry if I interrupted your thoughts, but I have a big problem."

"That would not be the first time," Doctor Phillips said.

"It's Sara, my grandmother. Someone kidnapped her. We just got her home. She's unresponsive."

"Well, let's get her in here," Doctor Phillips said curtly.

"No, no, we can't. It's a sensitive matter, and I can't go into detail. Will you please come and check her out?" Ann said.

"Do you know if she's had food or water?" Doctor Phillips asked.

"She was locked in the trunk of a car. I doubt that she's had food or water," Ann said.

"Let me get an IV pole and some liquid food. I'll be right back," Doctor Phillips said and started to walk away.

"Wait! Wait! Will you get an arm sleeve for a bruised arm?" Ann asked.

Doctor Phillips stared at her for a moment, and then said, "An arm sleeve for a bruised arm. Got it!" he said, and then he rushed away.

Ann waited for what seemed like an extraordinarily long time, but finally, Doctor Phillips returned carrying a large black leather bag and an IV pole.

"You're driving?" he said.

"Yes, shall I carry the bag?"

"No, I'm fine. You can still call me Noah," he said. "Let's hurry. It seems like Sara is in a bad way. Do you know if she has bananas and peanut butter at home?"

"I don't know. It's Grandmother's house. I don't know what she has," Ann said.

"Get me settled in at the house, and then you go get some bananas that are soft and not green, some natural peanut butter, and two gallons of distilled water. Get some pears if you can find some that are really ripe, and get kiwi, the riper the better. We'll mash them into a paste."

Ann drove to Sara's house, and they hurriedly got out of the car. Doctor Phillips grabbed the IV pole and leather bag, and they rushed into the house. Ann led Doctor Phillips to Sara's bedroom.

"Hello. Sorry we're meeting under these circumstances," Doctor Phillips said, looking at Kate and shaking her hand

"Please get the food and water," Doctor Phillips said, addressing Ann.

Ann got the arm sleeve from the bag and rushed out of the house and to her car. She drove to Kate's house, gave the arm sleeve to Molly with instructions to put it on Sally Sue's arm, got the food and water, and returned to Sara's house. She rushed inside, carrying what she had purchased, and met Doctor Phillips and Kate.

"Ann, I was just telling Kate. Sara needs to be in the hospital. There is no way we can provide adequate care for her here. She needs round-the-clock care and monitoring. We can't provide it here, but it's up to you and your mother."

Kate looked at Ann for a moment and said, "I agree. Do you have any objections, honey?"

"No, Mother, let's get her to the hospital," Ann said, and then she turned to Doctor Phillips. "Noah, uh…Doctor Phillips, can she have a private room?"

"I'll see what I can do. I'm calling for an ambulance as we speak, and a room."

As they waited for an ambulance, Doctor Phillips reserved a private room, ordered IV fluids that were specially formulated to counter the dehydration that had invaded her body, ordered additional fluids to feed her, and he ordered a heart monitor. Later, he would perform various tests to determine if any organs had been damaged, and he would focus especially on her mental faculties.

When the ambulance arrived, Kate rode with her mother to the hospital, and then she followed the gurney that was used to transport Sara to her private room.

Ann followed in her vehicle. After she was satisfied that Sara was in good care, she returned to Kate's house to relieve Molly and Cynthia.

"Molly and Cynthia, thank you for helping us out," Ann said. "Grandmother Sara is in the hospital because Sally Sue did some terrible things to her, so we're going to get Sally Sue well enough that we can turn her over to the authorities for punishment. Meanwhile, we have to keep her here until Grandmother gets well. How do we keep her under guard so that she doesn't get away?"

Molly and Cynthia looked at each other, and then they looked at Ann.

"We could tie a rope around her and keep her on the leash," Cynthia said.

Ann was silent for a moment, but then she said, "Are you thinking about letting her outside on a leash?"

Cynthia looked at Molly and then at Ann. "I don't know," she said.

"There's so much to think about. If we lock her up in a bedroom, she may choke herself with a sheet or pillow. If we lock her up in a room with nothing in it, we risk getting attacked when we open the door."

"What if we tie a rope around her waist with the knot in her back so she can't untie it. After that, take one loose end and tie one ankle, then take the other loose end and tie her other ankle but leave some loose rope. After she's tied, take the loose end and tie it to the back of the couch, the back of a chair, or any other place where she's at," Molly said.

"Oh, my gosh, Molly! You just did it! That's the answer! She can sit on the couch and watch TV for a coupla hours, and then we'll get her up, tie her hands behind her back and walk her around the house. We want her as healthy as she can be," Ann said.

"I'll make sure she don't get away," Cynthia said.

"I'm so satisfied. Thanks to the two of you, we're going to make this work," Ann said. "There is one more problem. My mother and I are going to take turns staying with Grandmother. So, how're all of us going to sleep and watch Sally Sue at the same time?"

"When are you trading with Kate?" Molly asked.

"Probably tonight," Ann said.

"Can you sleep at the hospital tonight because your grandmother will be sleeping?" Molly said.

Ann hesitated for a moment. "Of course, I can. Thank you, Molly. Now what about the two of you and Mother?"

"Kate's had a long night and day. As soon as she gets home, she can go to bed. Cynthia can go at eight o'clock. I'll wake her at two, and then I'll go to bed."

"Sounds like a plan. Before we start anything, I'm going out to get some rope. Do you and Cynthia want anything from the outside?" Ann asked Molly.

Acting timid, Molly said, "Can we get some milk and eggs? Oh, and some bread and bottled water?"

"Milk, eggs, bread, and water. Got it. I'm leaving. Text me if you have any problems or if you want something," Ann said.

"We will," Molly said.

Ann left the house, got in her car, and drove to the produce company where she got rope. She wasn't about to go to a store, buy rope, and leave a trail for the legal community to develop a big story about her family. After that, she stopped at a grocery store, got groceries for Molly, and returned to Kate's house. *It's time for me to relieve Mother,* she thought as she walked up the steps to the house.

Suddenly, the front door opened, and Molly came out. "I'll help you," she said.

"Good. Do you have everything under control?" Ann asked.

"Yes, ma'am."

"Okay, I'm off to the hospital to relieve Kate. I'll see you later," Ann said, and then she left the house and drove to the hospital. She parked and rushed into the building and down the hallway to Sara's room.

Kate looked up as Ann entered the room. Putting her forefinger to her lips, she got up and walked hurriedly to meet Ann. "Let's go out in the hall," she whispered.

They walked out of the room and into the hallway.

"How is she?" Ann asked.

"She's been lying still the entire night. She did whimper one time, and that's a plus, but she has a long way to go. I am so worried," Kate said.

"Remember, Mother. We're special. She'll be up calling for us to attend a meeting in no time at all. Please go home and get some rest. Molly and Cynthia have Sally Sue under control. Take my car," Ann said, handing her car keys to Kate. "The truck's down from the Emergency Room."

"I do need rest. I've been thinking about Sally Sue also. She has to have received calls on her cell phone. I'm going to charge it and check it and then I'm putting a tracker on it. We can never be too sure of ourselves," Kate said.

"Excellent idea," Ann said.

I'll see you tonight," Kate said. She took Ann's keys, left the hospital, drove home, went into her house, and met Molly. "How're things?" she asked.

"We have everything under control. Why don't you get some shut eye?" Molly said.

"I haven't slept in days. I'm so exhausted. I don't even know if I can sleep. What about you and Cynthia? You need sleep too," Kate said.

"We're going to switch out with each other. Cynthia will watch Sally Sue while I take a nap, and then I'll watch her while Cynthia naps. It's no big deal," Molly said.

"Okay, it all sounds good. I'm hitting the sack," Kate said, and then she left the room to go to her bedroom.

"Uh…uh, haf…bafroom," Sally Sue grunted.

Cynthia looked at Molly who immediately waved her hands, first gesturing toward Sally Sue and then at Cynthia.

"Take her," Molly said in a low tone of voice.

Cynthia shrugged her shoulders and sighed. "Help me untie her," she said.

"Uh…wa…watta," Sally Sue uttered.

"You want bafroom or water?" Cynthia said, her voice sounding irritated.

Sally Sue was quiet.

"Bafroom first," Cynthia said quickly. "If you're good, we'll think about water," she said, and then she untied her and held her upright as they struggled to get to the bathroom.

"I'm only doing this once," Cynthia said as she lifted Sally Sue's skirt and pulled down her underwear. "You get well or you have problems," Cynthia said.

Sally Sue finished, and Cynthia supported her until they reached the couch. She slumped down, and then Cynthia put the rope around her neck, made a slip knot, threw the other end over the couch, then back under the couch, and tied it to Sally Sue's feet. "That's the way I do it," Cynthia said.

For the next two days, Kate and Ann exchanged places at the hospital. The third day brought miraculous changes. Sara regained consciousness, took four steps as she was supported by Kate, and Sally Sue walked to the bathroom without support from anyone.

Days four and five brought even more remarkable changes. Sara was given permission to go home to recuperate, and Sally Sue was walking all over the house under close supervision by Cynthia.

During the early morning of day six, Sally Sue told Cynthia she was going to the bathroom. Cynthia, yawning and complaining about being awakened, still agreed to follow her to the bathroom.

"I need privacy. You stay out here," Sally Sue said.

"I can't do that," Cynthia said. "I'd get in big trouble."

"But I need privacy," Sally Sue insisted. "Besides, there's nowhere for me to go. Now, please, just stay outside the door."

"Okay, you do your business and come right back out. I'll be waitin' right here," Cynthis said.

"Just don't peep," Sally Sue said, and then she went into the bathroom and closed the door.

Cynthia yawned repeatedly and then sat down on the floor in front of the door and waited.

Ten minutes passed. "Sally Sue, I'm comin' in," Cynthia said, and then she opened the door and went inside. "Oh, no!" she shrieked as she backed out and away from the bathroom.

"What is it? What's wrong? Are you okay?" Molly said, her voice loud and sounding concerned as she ran to meet Cynthia.

Cynthia grabbed both of Molly's arms. "Gone! Gone!" she uttered, and then flailed her arms wildly pointing at the bathroom.

Reaching for Cynthia's arms, she held them steady for a few moments and then walked slowly into the bathroom. She immediately felt cooler air coming from the window that was situated near the shower stall. The windowpane had been removed, and Sally Sue was gone.

Molly jerked back and then ran to the bedroom where Kate slept. "Ms. Kate, Ms. Kate, please wake up," she said in a low but anxious voice, touching Kate's shoulder as she talked.

"Wha...wha...what's the matter?" Kate said, raising her head from the pillow.

"She's gone! Sally Sue's gone! She got out through the bathroom window," Molly said, her voice high-pitched and anxious.

Kate stared at her for a moment before saying anything. Finally, she said, "Don't worry, honey. We'll catch her." Getting her phone, she called Ann. The phone rang several times before Ann finally answered.

"Hel...hello," Ann said, her voice barely audible.

"Honey, Sally Sue escaped through the bathroom window. I'm going to get Mother, and then I'll come and get you. Please meet us outside. Bring the pulley and rope," Kate said, her anxious words coming fast. "Bring a hand towel too."

"I'll be ready," Ann said, her voice still low and muffled from just being awakened.

"I'll be back," Kate told Molly as she jerked on the clothes she had worn before going to bed. Rushing out of the house, she dialed Sara as she hurried to the car.

"Wha...wha...what is it," Sara uttered.

"Mother, we have to take a road trip. Sally Sue escaped. I'm on the way to pick you up, and I'm sorry, but we have to hurry."

"I'll be ready in two minutes," Sara said.

Kate picked up Sara and then drove to Ann's house. Ann stood outside holding a large leather bag which she put in the back seat of Kate's SUV.

"I'm ready. Good morning, Grandmother," Ann said.

"We have business to attend to," Sara said.

"Sally Sue thought to take her phone. Lucky for us, because I have a tracker on her phone," Kate said, a distinct smile crossing her face. "Oh, there she is headed west on Interstate 40. She must've stolen a car in our subdivision."

"Let's go get 'er," Sara said.

"We're off," Kate said, and then she drove a short distance and entered the interstate. "Honey, keep tracking her," she said and gave her phone to Ann.

"She's still going west," Ann said.

They drove for approximately thirty minutes, and then Ann said, "She's taking the exit just ahead. There's a service station there. Now, is she going inside for a drink or going to the bathroom?"

"She doesn't have any money, so I'll bet on the bathroom," Kate said.

"That'll be great. We can catch her on the way out," Ann said.

Kate took the exit that Sally Sue had taken. "There's only one car at the station," she said.

"That has to be Sally Sue," Ann said.

"You two watch for her to come out of the bathroom. I'll check out the inside," Sara said.

"Okay, let's do it," Kate said. She and Ann got out of the car and took up positions on each side of the bathroom door.

Five minutes passed, and then the door opened. A woman came out wearing the same skirt that Sally Sue wore at the bar nearly a week ago.

Kate and Ann moved seemingly in one motion, grabbing Sally Sue's arms.

"Hi, Sally Sue. What a surprise finding you here," Kate said.

Sally Sue twisted and tried to kick, but Kate and Ann held her tight.

"We're taking you to rehab," Kate said, and then they pulled Sally Sue to Kate's vehicle and put her in the back seat. Ann slid in on one side of her, and Sara opened the door and took up residence on her other side.

Sally Sue's eyes opened wide as she stared at Sara, who was once her captive.

Kate drove back through Nashville, east on Interstate 24, and then took an exit and drove north to a walking trail that bordered Percy Priest Lake.

"Okay, we're taking a break here," Kate said.

"Mother, can you and Grandmother walk beside Sally Sue? I have some luggage that I have to carry," Ann said.

"Why, of course, honey," Kate said. "Do you know where we're stretching our legs?"

"Yes, through that strand of trees. Lucky for us, daylight has started to move in," Ann said.

Sally Sue refused to walk, so Kate and Sara hooked their arms underneath her armpits and dragged her along.

They walked for ten minutes before Ann said, "I'm going on ahead. You have about five more minutes to walk." She looked at Kate and then at Sara.

"Okay, dear. Be careful," Kate said.

Ann ran ahead holding her leather bag. A few moments passed, and she stopped at the base of a tree that grew on an embankment that overlooked Percy Priest Lake. "It's perfect," she said, and then she removed the pulley and rope from the leather bag. Holding the rope loosely in one hand, she threw one end over a tree branch that grew out over the water. Holding a six-foot length of rope, she held the pulley and climbed the tree to the branch that held the rope she had thrown across earlier.

"You are so nice," she said as she looked up at a tree branch that grew parallel with the branch that held the rope. She took the six-foot length of rope, threw one end over the tree limb, and then securely tied the pulley. She then took one end of the long rope and threaded it through the pulley and threw the loose end of the rope down to the ground. The other end of the rope lay loosely on the ground.

"We're here," Kate said.

"Good. I'm going to put this around Sally Sue, so she won't fall in the water," Ann said, and then she put one end of the rope underneath

Sally Sue's armpits, routed it to her backside, and tied a slipknot. She hurried to get the second end of the rope and wrapped it around a tree that was part of the grove of trees where everyone stood. She pulled the hand towel from the leather bag, climbed back to Sally Sue, and tied the hand towel around her face covering her mouth. She climbed down and got to the other end of the rope. Pulling on the rope until she felt Sally Sue's resistance on the other end, she said, "I'm ready."

Kate walked to where Ann stood. "Pull her up," Kate said. "Let me check, and I'll be right back."

A few moments later, Kate returned and said, "Let the rope down very slowly."

As Ann managed the rope, Sara stood looking up at Sally Sue, who was held by the rope and was descending slowly toward the water.

"You have been an evil person," Sara said to Sally Sue. "Today, as you descend toward your destiny, I want you to remember your helpless children as you held them down in the bathwater. You watched them as they suffocated under your hands. They were defenseless, but you didn't care. You snuffed out their lives without any mercy or conscience. Today, you will meet the same fate as you provided them. You will leave this earth slowly and painfully. You chose this path."

Sally Sue flailed wildly from side to side. Her screams were muffled by the hand towel. She seemed in slow motion as she entered the water still twisting viciously from side to side. The water splashed until her head was submerged. Several moments passed, and it became still.

Kate walked back and forth between Sara and Ann. A number of moments passed. Finally, she said, "Pull her up."

Ann pulled the rope. It was heavier than before.

Finally, Kate told her, "That's good. It's over. Let's go home."

Sara joined them, and they began walking back through the grove of trees toward their vehicle.

"This would be a good place to have a picnic," Sara said.

EPILOGUE

"Ladies, I have asked you to visit me for a very special reason," Sara said, and then she hesitated and looked at Kate and Ann to make sure she had their attention. "We have earned a large amount of currency in our apprehension of some of the most rotten people on earth. Now, at least one-third of that will go to the government simply because we have the courage, the fortitude, and the initiative to do dirty work, and the government wants to prosper from our sweat and labor.

"I want to propose something that may shock you, although both of you come from strong stock. I'm still concerned that you'll fall over in your chairs.

"Everyone still with me?"

"Of course, Mother. You have our full attention," Kate said.

"You sure have my attention," Ann said.

"That's good. That's really good. Okay, here's what's on my mind. Why don't we share some of this currency…not with anyone but with little kids who have been stricken with disease?"

Kate looked at Ann, who looked back and shrugged.

"That sounds…well, we both think…that is, agree…well, that's a wonderful plan…I mean idea," Kate said, and then she looked at Ann. "Don't you think so, honey?"

"I do think…I mean…well, yes, what a plan! Or idea…yes, idea, that fits it."

Sara looked at them for a few moments. "Well, I can see I caught you two off balance."

"Oh, no, Mother. We're just…well, we were just thinking…I mean we were waiting for the details," Kate said.

"Details, huh? Well, part of the details would be a generous gift to St. Jude Children's Hospital," Sara said.

"St. Jude, a very nice gesture…I mean a very worthy cause," Kate said.

Sara cleared her throat, looked at Kate, and then at Ann, and said, "And the Shriner's Hospital would be another one."

"That's a very nice one," Ann said, and then she looked at her mother for affirmation.

"I agree. It's a very good choice," Kate said.

"Good. I'm happy that we all agree with the direction that I'm steering this ship," Sara said. "Wha…what is that? The doorbell."

"I'll get it, Mother," Kate said, and then she walked hurriedly to the front door and opened it.

"Sara Patterson?" a man in uniform asked.

"Uh…no, no, I'll get her," Kate said.

"I'll go with you," the police officer said as he followed Kate into the house.

Two other men followed behind them.

Kate walked to the living room, pointed to Sara, and said, "That's my mother, Sara Patterson. "

"I have a warrant for your arrest, ma'am," the first officer said.

"A warrant? You have a warrant for me?" Sara asked, dumbfounded.

"Yes, ma'am," the officer said.

"What kind of warrant is it?" Sara asked.

"A warrant for murder. I'm going to have to take you downtown," the officer said.

Sara stared at him for an uncomfortable moment but finally said, "And what if I don't want to go?"

"Then we'd have to forcefully take you."

"In handcuffs?"

"Not if I can help it. If you'll cooperate, I won't handcuff you now, but when we get downtown, I'll have to put handcuffs on you."

"Ladies, it looks like I'm going downtown," Sara said.

"We'll go with you, Mother," Kate said.

"Oh, no, ladies. We're taking Sara and no one else," the officer said.

"What will happen to her?" Ann asked.

"She will be confined until the prosecutor decides to convene a grand jury or present his case directly to the court," the officer said.

"Confined! Where will she be…as you put it…confined?" Kate asked.

"That I don't know. We're taking her downtown, that's all I know, and we have to go. Let's go, ma'am," the officer said, looking at Sara.

"Let me get my purse," Sara said.

"You won't need your purse where you're going. Please follow me," the officer ordered, and then he started walking toward the door.

"Follow him," one of the officers said.

Sara followed the first officer, and the other two officers followed her.

Kate and Ann followed the procession out of the house and watched as Sara was put in the back seat of one of the police cruisers with one officer sitting on her left side and one on her right side.

"Mother, we've been betrayed," Ann said.

"We're not betrayed for very long. Let's go see Chief Martin and get this thing straightened out," Kate said.

"I'll drive. Do we go to city hall?"

"I would think that's where the chief would be. Let's go, honey. Mother must be thinking terrible thoughts just about now."

They left the house, and Ann drove them to city hall where they parked and went inside.

"'Police Department', that's what we're looking for," Kate said.

They went inside and walked to a desk manned by an officer with two stripes on his shirt. As they approached the desk, the officer neither moved nor raised his head. He seemed intent on watching something on his telephone.

Kate cleared her throat, but the officer continued looking at his phone.

"Excuse me, sir," Kate said.

The officer did not acknowledge her.

"Excuse me, sir. We have a question," Kate said.

"Yeah?" the officer grunted.

"We're looking for Chief Martin," Kate said.

"He ain't here," the officer said as he continued to gaze at his phone.

"He's not here? Where can we find him?" Kate asked.

"He's not with the force anymore. Well, as far as I know," the officer said, his words coming slowly.

"He's not with the police department anymore?" Kate sounded stunned. "Who can tell us where he went?"

"I wouldn't know," the officer said, still intently engrossed in his phone.

"Will you call someone who might know…maybe your captain?" Kate said.

"Ain't nobody here but me," the officer responded.

Kate looked at Ann and appeared exasperated.

"What about Sara Patterson? She was just brought in by three officers."

"Okay," the officer said in a drawling voice.

"Officer, would you please look at us?" Ann said. "We have something to ask you."

Slowly, as if he were operating with a broken neck, the officer raised his head and looked at Kate and Ann. His eyes traveled in slow motion from their faces, down their bodies, and then returned to their faces. "What can I do for you ladies?"

Starting to talk simultaneously, Ann said, "I'm sorry, Mother. Go ahead."

"We're looking for Sara Patterson. She was brought here by three officers within the past thirty minutes."

"She ain't here," the officer said.

Kate looked at Ann. Her face reflected her exasperation.

"Can you tell me where she is?" Kate asked.

"You might try the Wilson County Justice Building in Lebanon," the officer said, his words spaced so that his sentence took an unusually long period of time to complete.

"Let's go, honey," Kate said. She and Ann walked out of the building without further communication with the officer. As they walked across the parking lot and got into Ann's car, Kate said, "Let's go to the justice building."

"Let me get directions," Ann said, and then she requested directions from her phone. "Okay, we're going up Highway 70."

"You know, we haven't the foggiest idea what we're doing, what we're going to do, and how we're going to do it," Kate said. "If mother is charged with murder, and we can't find Chief Martin, we have a serious problem."

"I know, Mother. We haf to find the chief. The agreement that he had with Grandmother will exonerate her without a doubt. Didn't he clear the agreement with the state legislature?" Ann said.

"As I remember, the legislature was to validate the agreement with the chief and Mother and issue a written declaration to that effect. The problem is that I don't know if that was ever done, and I don't know if Mother knows. We have to talk with her, and there's no maybes or buts, we have to talk with her," Kate said.

"Do you think we should talk with an attorney?" Ann asked.

"It might come to that. We first need to talk with a bondsman, I think," Kate suggested.

"Why don't we see the bondsman as soon as we talk with Grandmother?"

"We will. I think we're here, honey, and there's a place to park."

Ann parked, and they went inside the building that had "Wilson County Criminal Justice Center" emblazoned across the front.

"Let's go talk with the officer behind the counter," Kate said.

They walked to the counter where an officer was looking through several pages of paper.

"Officer, we're relatives of Sara Patterson. Would she happen to be here?" Kate said.

"Well, let's see," the officer said, and then he began looking through the sheets of paper. "Yes, we do have a Sara Patterson."

"May we see her, please?" Kate said.

"Lady, no one sees her except her attorney," the officer said.

"But she's my mother, and this is her grandchild," Kate said, pointing to Ann.

"Like I said, lady, no one sees her except her attorney."

"Can we talk with your supervisor?" Kate asked.

"Lady, the captain, my supervisor, is busy, and he would tell you the same thing that I just told you. You won't be able to see Ms. Patterson until after she goes before the judge."

Kate turned to look at Ann. Her face was drawn, and she appeared to be at wit's end.

"Let's go, Mother. We have to see a bondsman," Ann said.

The officer looked at Ann with a strange expression, but he didn't speak.

"I saw a bail bondsman sign just before we got here. It's only a block away," Kate said.

"Well, let's go make bail for Grandmother then," Ann said.

They left the justice center and went to the bail bond office that Kate had seen.

"How can I help you two ladies?" a large, heavily built man with a white beard asked.

"We came to make bail for my mother and Ann's grandmother," Kate said.

Realizing her statement needed clarification, she said, "My mother and Ann's grandmother are the same woman. This is Ann. She's my daughter," Kate explained, and then she smiled slightly.

"Whew, I'm glad we cleared that up. My name's Bo, by the way. Some people call me Bo Bail. They think it's funny, but I'm not too keen on it, if you want to know the truth. Now, back to your mother and Ann's grandmother. How much is her bail?"

Kate looked at Ann and then back at Bo. "Well, we don't know. How do we find that out?"

"You ladies have never been to court, have you? I can tell. It just radiates off a person sometimes."

"No. All this is new to us," Kate said.

"What was your name again?" Bo asked, looking at Kate.

"I'm sorry. I'm not sure if I even gave it to you," Kate said and smiled. "My name's Kate, and I gave you Ann's name."

"Okay, now that we got that squared away, Kate and Ann, here's how this thing works. Your mother will probably go before a judge, and your mother will plead guilty or not guilty. If she pleads not guilty, the judge will set bail. That's when you come and see me. So, until your mother sees the judge, there's nothing we can do to help her.

"Now, can I help you with anything else?"

Kate and Ann looked at each other, and then Kate said, "No, thank you. Well, yes," she said quickly. "How long does it take for someone to see the judge?"

"Oh, now, that's a good one. You know, of course, that the court system is backed up to the moon. Why, they're not even over Covid yet. I suspect you're looking at six to seven months before your mother sees the judge."

"Six to seven months!" Ann said loudly.

"Oh yeah, Miss. It's a long drawn-out affair," Bo said.

"Honey, let's go. I'm sure Bo has more fish to fry than just us," Kate said.

Ann looked at Bo and then at Kate. "Okay, Mother."

They walked back to Ann's car in silence. Once inside the car, Kate said, "We've got to see someone higher…maybe the attorney general…"

"Now, that's an idea," Ann said, "and he's in Nashville. Should we make an appointment with him?"

"No, we'd just get put off. Let's jump in front of the line and just show up. We need to help Mother today and not a minute later."

"Mother, you are terrific. I'm so glad you're my mother," Ann said.

"Shhh. Not so loud. I'm enamored with the thoughts of people thinking we're sisters."

Ann laughed.

"Do you know that's the first laugh we've had since this nightmare started?" Kate said.

"We're going to solve this, Mother. Remember, we have that special spirit that opens doors for us."

"Thank you for reminding me. Let's get on the interstate and burn rubber," Kate said.

Ann laughed again. "Yes, ma'am, we're going to make this happen."

"Do we know where the attorney general is located?" Kate asked.

"Very near the Capitol on Fifth Avenue," Ann said.

"How do you know that?" Kate said.

"We sell produce to the cafeteria," Ann said.

Kate laughed. "Now, what you just said a minute ago is truer than you ever imagined."

"You mean about the spirit in our life?" Ann said.

"Yes, we are watched over like a batch of baby chicks. You sell produce to the attorney general. How sweet is that?"

Ann drove to Fifth Avenue and parked in a nearby parking garage, and then they walked to the State Government Office where the attorney general had his office.

"Let's go to the left. There are less steps to climb on that side," Kate said.

"Mother, you need steps to keep you healthy," Ann said. "We have to go through security. There's nothing in your purse to frighten them, I hope."

"No, I left my revolver at home," Kate said.

They walked up the steps to the building, went through security, and then walked to the information desk.

"May I help you?" an attractive, blonde-haired woman said.

"Uh, we're here to see the attorney general," Kate said.

A puzzled look crossed the woman's face, and she hesitated for a few moments. "Do you have an appointment with the attorney general?" she asked.

"No, we thought we might be able to see him only for a minute or so. We have a very critical matter to discuss with him," Kate said.

"I'm the receptionist. My name's Suzanne. May I have the nature of the matter? I may be able to help."

Kate looked at Ann and then turned back to the receptionist. "Well, it's about my mother and Ann's grandmother…this is Ann," she said, pointing to Ann, "and I'm Kate. You see, she's…my mother, that is, she's been arrested, and we're trying to post bail so she can come home."

"I see," the receptionist said. "This sounds like a matter that the Division of Consumer Affairs could handle."

"Oh, I don't think so," Kate said. "This is a criminal matter. We need to talk with the attorney general," she said.

The receptionist paused for a moment, looked down at her desk, then at the computer, and finally said. "I think I know just the person who can help you. Let's see if she's available," she said, and then she rang someone on her phone. "Hi, Ms. Wimpley. I have two citizens at my desk that have a problem. Can you spare a moment to answer a question for them?" the receptionist said, and then she held the phone for a moment. "Oh, thank you. I will let them know," she said, and then she looked at Kate and said, "Ms. Wimpley will be right out."

"Who is Ms. Wimpley?" Ann asked.

"Oh, she's over the Criminal Division. She's an attorney and very smart," the receptionist said.

Kate and Ann looked at each other but didn't move from their position until a large-framed woman with a stern-looking face and gray hair approached them. She walked with authority, and every step on the flooring caused an uncomfortable sound that seemingly vibrated against the hallway walls and hung around until the next step.

"Whom am I talking with?" she asked the receptionist with a deep, authoritarian voice.

"Oh, Ms. Wimpley, this is Kate and her daughter, Ann."

"What can I do for you?" Ms. Wimpley said without changing any facial expression.

"Uh, it's my mother and Ann's grandmother. She's been charged with murder, and she's completely innocent. We need to post bail for her, but no one will tell us how much the bail is," Kate said.

"Miss—that is, Kate—you need to engage an attorney. We don't get involved with personal matters at this level. I cannot recommend an attorney for you. Good luck to you," Ms. Wimpley said, and then she turned and walked away.

Kate and Ann appeared stunned. They stood silently for a few moments, and then Kate said, "Let's go, honey."

They walked away from the receptionist's desk hurriedly, past security, and out the front door.

"Mother, it looks like we're going to haf to handle this ourselves," Ann said.

Kate stopped, which caused Ann to stop. They looked at each other for a few moments, and then Kate said, "Yes, it does, honey."

OTHER BOOKS BY BRYCE THUNDER KING

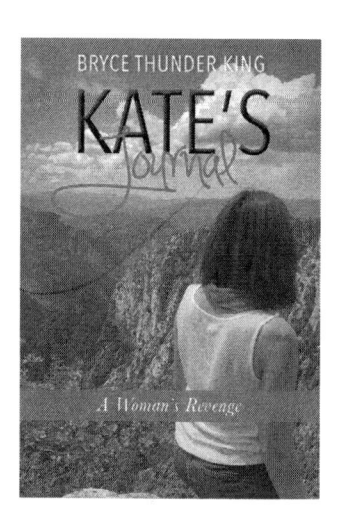

KATE'S JOURNAL: A WOMAN'S REVENGE (BOOK 1)

At a tender age, Kate's mother delivers a chilling prophecy at the dinner table: her father will soon fall gravely ill, and Kate must remain silent and emotionless, no matter how distressing it becomes. Just days after his death, her mother reveals an even darker lesson—teaching Kate how to mix a deadly potion and warning her to never let any man abuse her.

As Kate grows into a striking young woman with fiery red hair, she catches the eye of men like Mark, the mayor, and Ken—each unaware of the venomous cunning lurking beneath her beauty. But when Kate's anger toward Ken leads her to a fatal mistake, she finds herself locked away in Nashville Women's Prison, a pawn to the ruthless warden. Will she find a way to outsmart her captor and escape, or will she sink deeper into the darkness of her own making?

The clock is ticking, and Kate's true power has only just begun to reveal itself.

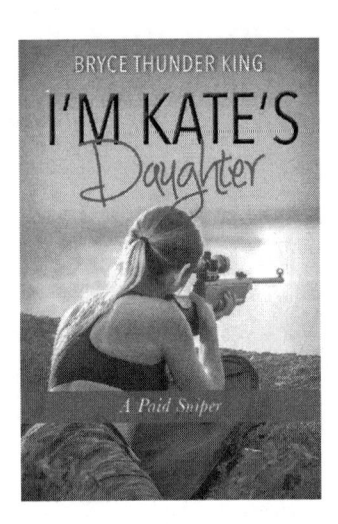

I'M KATE'S DAUGHTER: A PAID SNIPER (BOOK 2)

When Ann visits her mother, she expects a quiet family gathering. But when her best friend, Cynthia, is brutally attacked on her way home, Ann's world tilts into darkness. Fueled by rage, she seeks out Frankie Santini—a dangerous man with the power to help her take revenge.

Frankie agrees, but there's a price: Ann must become his sniper. She signs the deal with the devil, trading her old life for twenty high-stakes missions and twenty-eight kills. But when she wants out, the devil won't let her go so easily. With a hit on her head and nowhere safe to turn, Ann vanishes—leaving behind her money, identity, and past. She disappears into the shadows, blending with the homeless along the Cumberland River. But Ann isn't just running. She's a predator in hiding.

Because Ann isn't like everyone else.

Ann is a psychopath.